PENGUIN BOOKS

Oberammergau and the Passion Play

James Bentley

Oberammergau

and the Passion Play

Penguin Books

Penguin Books Ltd, Harmondsworth, Middlesex, England
Penguin Books, 40 West 23rd Street, New York, New York 10010, U.S.A.
Penguin Books Australia Ltd, Ringwood, Victoria, Australia
Penguin Books Canada Ltd, 2801 John Street, Markham, Ontario, Canada L3R 1B4
Penguin Books (N.Z.) Ltd, 182–190 Wairau Road, Auckland 10, New Zealand

First published 1984

Designed by Michael Scott
Made and printed in Great Britain by
Butler & Tanner Ltd, Frome, Somerset
Set in 10/11½pt Monophoto Plantin

TO AUDREY,
REMEMBERING OUR OBERAMMERGAU HOLIDAYS

Acknowledgements

As always, I am grateful to the staff of the libraries in which I have worked – the British Library, the John Rylands University Library, Manchester, and the Bodleian – and, in the case of this book, especially to the staff of the Wiener Library in London.

I am grateful for permission to work in the archive of Thomas Cook in London, and particularly grateful to Mr F.T. Emere who gave me considerable help when I was there.

Finally, I want to thank Elizabeth and Charles Handy for looking after me when I was writing part of this book in their Norfolk home.

James Bentley
1983

Acknowledgement is made to the following for illustrations used in the text:

J. Allan Cash (pages 16, 20, 21, 26, 27, 65, 66 (*right*), 87, Plate 13); Colour Library International (Plate 16); Thomas Cook (pages 84, 85); Foto-Huber (Plates 1–12); Mansell Collection (Pages 8, 14 (*right*), 18 (*top*), 19 (*top*), 24, 35, 57, 67 (*left*), 68 (*top*), 70, 81); Mary Evans Picture Library (pages 15, 31, 34, 45); Werner Neumeister (Plates 14, 15, 18); Popperfoto (pages 11, 14 (*left*), 17, 18 (*bottom*), 19 (*bottom*), 22, 23, 28, 29, 30, 32, 33, 44, 46, 47, 48, 49, 50, 51, 52, 55, 58, 61, 63, 64, 66 (*left*), 67 (*right*), 68 (*bottom*), 69, 71, 79, 82, 83, 86, 89); Toni Schneiders (Plate 17).

Contents

1 The Vow

In the year 1632 the plague came to Oberammergau. It came stealthily, overnight, from the neighbouring village of Eschenlohe.

The plague had reached Bavaria as a result of war. 1617 was the centenary year of the Protestant Reformation in Germany, but Catholics and Protestants had not yet learned to live together peacefully. Banded together with their allies either in the Protestant Union or the Catholic League, countries as far apart as Sweden and Spain threatened each other. In 1618 Protestants in Bohemia were denied the right to meet together. The Bohemian nobles responded by flinging out of a fortress window in Prague two ministers of the Catholic Emperor, together with a private secretary. This 'defenestration of Prague' started a war which lasted for thirty years.

The rulers of Catholic Bavaria naturally threw in their lot with the imperial Habsburgs. For some years all went well. Under the leadership of a Walloon, General Tilly, the forces of the Catholic League succeeded in taking Bohemia from the Protestants. Then, on 21 September 1631, King Gustavus Adolphus of Sweden defeated Tilly's army at the battle of Breitenfeld.

The victorious Protestants pressed on towards Bavaria. Before the end of the year they had stormed and captured Würzburg. Tilly was finally and completely crushed in a battle on the River Lech, and on 17 May 1632 Gustavus Adolphus took Munich.

Although marauding soldiers roamed most of Bavaria, Oberammergau escaped the slaughter. In June 1632 a gang of these soldiers plundered the neighbouring monastery of Ettal, killing two of the monks and sacking buildings. Other villages were attacked, their inhabitants killed and robbed. 'You would not recognize our poor Bavaria,' wrote the Elector Maximilian. 'Villages and convents have gone up in flames, priests, monks and citizens have been tortured and killed at Fürstenfeld, at Diessen, at Benediktbeuren and in the Ettal.' Gustavus Adolphus was accused of wishing to destroy the ruler of Bavaria at the expense of his subjects and their livelihood. 'With God's help,' he wrote to his allies in Bohemia, 'we shall be able to limit his power and do away with it in his own lands through their total ruin.'

In this war of almost unprecedented savagery, the plague flourished. Plagues and epidemics had threatened men's lives as long as anyone could remember. The free imperial city of Augsburg for many years kept precise records of their ravages. In the first half of the sixteenth century, plagues had carried off 38,500 people in that one city alone. In the second half of the century, plagues killed 20,500. In the first half of the seventeenth century, they killed 34,000.

It is scarcely ever possible to say precisely whether any one such plague was the manifestation of a disease known to modern medicine. Some epidemics were transmitted by black rats. Typhoid was communicated through contaminated drinking water. A variety of typhoid that started with heart quakes, bouts of fever and terrible thirst broke out into black glandular boils, hence the name 'bubonic plague'. In the sixteenth century a new sort of plague was given the name *morbus novus*.

Few could even guess at the causes of such epidemics, but all knew their deadly symptoms. Daniel Defoe's *A Journal of the Plague Year*, describing the terror of 1665, provides a graphic account of the helplessness of the English before this kind of disease. The doctors themselves, Defoe observes, were helpless. Indeed, 'Abundance of quacks too died, who had the folly to trust to their own medicines, which they must needs be conscious to themselves were good for nothing.'

The plague attacked suddenly and terrifyingly. Defoe's narrator describes a woman who decided to put her daughter to bed, since the girl was suffering violent headaches and vomiting. While the bed was airing the mother undressed her daughter and discovered the marks of the plague on her body. The mother could do nothing but weep with grief. 'As to the young maiden, she was a dead corpse from that moment, for the gangrene which occasions the spots had spread over her whole body, and she died.' Defoe's narrator explained how the plague struck in different ways. 'Some were immediately overwhelmed with it, and it came to violent fevers, vomitings, insufferable headaches, pains in the back, and so up to ravings and ragings with those pains; others with swellings and tumours in the neck or groin or armpits, which till they could be broke put them into insufferable agonies and torments; while others, as I have observed, were silently infected, the fever preying upon their spirits insensibly, and they seeing little of it till they fell into swooning, and faintings, and death without pain.'

No one was immune. Earlier in the century John Donne, the sombre Dean of St Paul's, observed that robbers 'broke into houses, and seeking the wardrobes of others, found their own winding sheet, in the infection of that house, where they stole their own death'. Throughout Europe men and women, conscious that they were doomed by the disease, would often crazily roam the streets, deliberately infecting others. Those who were unavoidably obliged to go out of doors would walk down the centre of the street, hoping to avoid the plague by smelling or even chewing fragrant roots or herbs. The dead were buried in communal graves at least six feet deep. Defoe's narrator saw one grave in Áldgate churchyard fifteen or sixteen feet wide, forty feet long and in places twenty feet deep. Corpses no longer remained in church overnight before burial. Children were forbidden to approach dead bodies. Public burials ceased.

Such scourges occurred in times of peace. In times of war, populations were infinitely more vulnerable. Sanitation scarcely existed at the best of times. (The three men thrown through the window in Prague in 1618 escaped with their lives because they fell into a midden immediately outside the castle wall!) War made matters worse, and the Thirty Years' War worst of all. The unpaid armies roaming Europe lived, it has been

The village of Oberammergau, dominated by its Passion Play theatre

calculated, on a mere 1,700 calories a day, most of which they took from the inhabitants of the countries they were despoiling. For one week an army commanded by Wallenstein lived on nothing but fruit, every man suffering appalling dysentery. In such conditions the plague flourished as it had not done for three hundred years. The starving populations offered little resistance to it. 'The harvest of 1632 promised well, but in Bavaria and Swabia the passing troops trampled it down,' wrote C.V. Wedgwood; 'in Bavaria there was neither corn left to grind nor seed to sow for the year to come; plague and famine wiped out whole villages, mad dogs attacked their masters, and the authorities posted men with guns to shoot down the raving victims before they could contaminate their fellows.'

In that year one million people died of famine and the plague in Saxony alone. 'One may wander ten miles and see no living man or beast, save perchance one old man or a child or two old women,' wrote a contemporary, describing Württemberg. 'In all the villages the huts are full of corpses: man and wife, children, apprentices, sheep and oxen, slain by disease and hunger, eaten by wolves and foxes, crows and ravens, for there was none to bury them.' Württemberg had 400,000 inhabitants when the Thirty Years' War began and only 48,000 when it was over.

The worst years were those between 1627 and 1635, when six separate epidemics caused 29,865 deaths in Augsburg alone. And in all this the village of Oberammergau seemed to have escaped unscathed.

The village Council set about protecting the inhabitants by desperate measures. All day long armed men guarded its borders. Flares burned throughout the night, in order to light up anyone who might be attempting to enter. By midsummer 1632 the plague had reached Eschenlohe, only three miles away. In nearby Kohlgrub, a plaque on the church wall records that not a single house had escaped the plague and only two couples remained free from infection. These two couples promised, if only they continued to be spared, to restore the church, as (they said) would their descendants once every hundred years.

In autumn 1632 the Oberammergauers, still mercifully free from the plague, decided to go ahead with the annual celebration of the consecration of their village church. This festival usually took three days. Clearly the roving pedlars who were accustomed to sell their wares during the anniversary celebrations would be kept out this year. But the village could rejoice at its continued good fortune.

In plague-stricken Eschenlohe a native of Oberammergau, Kaspar Schisler, had been working on the farm of a landowner named Mayr when the village from which he came decided to put itself in a state of siege. Eschenlohe today is still a tiny, peaceful hamlet. The Germans in this region say 'the smaller the village, the finer the church', and Eschenlohe parish church certainly bears out the proverb. In the eighteenth century it was sumptuously restored, partly to a plan by the Munich court architect Johann Michael Fischer, but the restorers kept some of the treasures of the older church. These include a small picture of St Sebastian, elaborately framed, on the south wall near the high altar. In the past St Sebastian had been revered for his ability to protect men and women from the plague: the Romans credited him with halting an outbreak of plague in A.D. 680. A French pageant in his honour still survives, first performed in the year 1497 at Chalon-sur-Saône after he had, by his intercession, saved that village from infection. But in 1632 Eschenlohe had entreated the saint in vain.

Kaspar Schisler, however, bore no signs of the disease. He decided to return home for the Oberammergau church festival. Overnight he crept into the village. Tradition has it that he lived on the edge of Oberammergau; perhaps, too, the guards were slack, in view of the church festivities. In any case, Schisler would have known how to elude them, and he returned to his home and family. He brought the plague with him.

The Oberammergau chronicle of 1733 records that Kaspar Schisler returned to Eschenlohe to die, though other accounts say that he died in Oberammergau. Then his wife died, followed by his children. It is not possible to say how many others died too. The parish burial registers for 1632 and 1633 are incomplete, and in any case they never recorded the names of dead children at this time. Among those who are named as having succumbed was the parish priest, Primus Christeiner, one of the first to suffer in 1632. His successor was not easy to find, and no one bothered to enter many names until Marcellus Fatiga came to take Christeiner's place. Then he too died. Not surprisingly, the church verger, Hans Stükhl, unavoidably in contact with the dead, soon caught the infection and followed the two parish priests to the grave.

By 28 October 1632, the feast-day of St Simon and St Jude, eighty-four adults are known to have died of the plague in the small village of Oberammergau. By the following July the village Council decided to act.

Ignorant of the real sources of the plague, men and women in the seventeenth century often attributed epidemics to the supernatural. People saw ghosts walking over gravestones and had visions of hands with flaming swords coming out of the clouds. Sometimes men or women were accused of having made a pact with the devil, agreeing to spread the plague. Witnesses claimed to have seen them actually talking to Satan with this purpose in mind.

Others attributed the plague to the hand of God himself. 'War, pestilence and famine are the three scourges of God' was a seventeenth-century saying. In either case, whether sent by God or by the devil, the plague might be averted by an appeal to God. Daniel Defoe's narrator in his account of the plague year opened his Bible at random and read Psalm 91: 'Thou shalt not be afraid for the terror by night; nor for the arrow that flieth by day; nor for the pestilence that walketh in darkness, nor for the destruction that wasteth at noonday. A thousand shall fall at thy side, and ten thousand at thy right hand; but it shall not come nigh thee, only with thine eyes shalt thou behold and see the reward of the wicked. Because thou hast made the Lord, which is my refuge, even the most High, thy habitation, there shall no evil befall thee, neither shall any plague come by thy dwelling.'

Clearly those who faithfully trusted in God might hope to escape the plague. In Bavaria many believed that intercession by certain saints was especially efficacious against the plague. Eschenlohe trusted in St Sebastian. St Ulrich of Augsburg was reputed to offer protection against plagues borne by rats and mice. St Coloman, it was believed, could drive away the plague.

As the pathetic promise to restore Kohlgrub church, made by the four surviving villagers, reveals, the traditional manner of appealing to God was to promise to serve him henceforth in some special way. The village of Oberammergau made its own particular vow. In July 1633 the village Council led all those who could still walk in procession to the parish church. There before the altar the Oberammergauers solemnly vowed that if God would rid them of this plague, they would for ever enact a Passion Play recalling the last week of Christ's life on earth, his crucifixion and his resurrection.

The plague was lifted, even though, as the chronicle records, some of the villagers already had its marks on their faces and bodies. From that moment no one else died of the disease in Oberammergau.

The Oberammergauers fulfilled their vow for the first time the following year. War still threatened them. A church account-book for 1635 notes that the villagers had to pay to repair the church chest after the Swedes had broken into the building. In that year, too, the invading Protestants forced the region round Ettal to pay a regular tax in return for an end to the repeated attacks they had suffered. But in spite of such hardships, the people of Oberammergau remained faithful to their vow. They had resolved to perform the Passion Play every ten years, and a

(*left*) Peter Rendel, St Peter in 1930, in his workshop

(*right*) Mary in 1934 – Anni Rutz, working before the *Kachelöfen*

second one took place in 1644. To this day they have kept their vow – though the wars that have continued to ravage Europe have at times forced the villagers to postpone, and on rare occasions cancel, performances of their play.

Four years later the Thirty Years' War came to an end. 'At the beginning of the sixteenth century,' observed the historian H.A.L. Fisher, 'Germany stood at the forefront of European civilization. By the end of the Thirty Years' War the country was barren of literature and art, burdened by an almost unmanageable language, and in its social manners and customs sunk to a Muscovite barbarity.'

Yet without this barbaric war the Oberammergauers would never have made their solemn vow. And without that vow it is doubtful whether the Oberammergau Passion Play would have survived to this day. In the sixteenth and seventeenth centuries such plays were common in Bavaria. Until the mid nineteenth century other Bavarian villages – Brixlegg, Kohlgrub, Mittelwald – still performed them. Only the Oberammergau Passion Play survives. In 1984, three hundred and fifty years after the first performance in gratitude for God's mercy, the people of Oberammergau are honouring their vow for the thirty-seventh time.

2 Keeping the Vow

In 1871 the future King Edward VII of England was at the Oberammergau Passion Play with his wife Princess Alexandra. Ironically, on his return to England in October he caught typhoid as a result of foul drains while staying with Lady Londesborough at Londesborough Lodge, Scarsborough, and almost died. A fellow guest, Lord Chesterfield, did in fact die of the disease.

The presence of the Prince and Princess of Wales at a Passion Play accords with our present-day notions of Oberammergau during the Passion Play seasons – filled with visitors, some of them well-known figures of theatre, literature or politics, many from other lands, all brought by the fame which faithfulness to the vow of 1633 has given this small village. But this picture is misleading if it is thought to apply to much of Oberammergau's earlier history. The Oberammergau Passion Play became famous only in the last century. Before that, the villagers

Oberammergau and its Passion Play theatre in 1860. As yet the actors and the set are completely uncovered. Behind is the peak of Kofel, with its huge cross. In view of the length of the performance, food was provided in stalls set up outside the theatre

kept their holy vow by performing it by themselves for themselves. Even as late as 1860 a visitor from abroad would notice that most of the crowd watching the Passion Play were local inhabitants, drawn also from surrounding villages – farmers, peasants, innkeepers, wood-carvers, housewives, butchers, and so on.

A visitor today would also be wrong in supposing that he is privileged, in the twentieth century, to be watching a medieval mystery play recreated at Oberammergau. The notion has misled distinguished men and women. In 1850 a famous German actor-manager, Eduard Devrient (the man who was responsible for reviving Bach's St Matthew Passion) was entranced at Oberammergau by what he called 'this precious survival from Old Germany'. As a great lover of his own nation and its traditions, Devrient proclaimed that the Oberammergau Passion Play 'rises before us, perfect in its old German atmosphere, as fresh and alive as if it had

Twentieth-century 'air painting' continues the old traditions

been conceived yesterday; its innocence, its untroubled childhood joy, seems to say to all of us, "Be of good cheer. The ancient stream of folk-art in Germany is inexhaustible."'

Devrient's praise helped to make Oberammergau and its Passion Play famous. But he was wrong about the play itself. By his time it was no longer the same drama that the villagers performed when they first kept their vow in 1634. That had certainly been a late medieval Passion Play. Almost certainly the villagers had performed such plays before 1634; they did not become overnight a skilled theatrical company. The story of Good Friday had been performed in Europe, first in Latin and then in the vernacular (often in local dialect), since the thirteenth century at least. In 1634 the Oberammergauers had a play ready to hand in order to keep their vow.

One of the splendid painted houses of Oberammergau. The artists loved to give the illusion of perspective

They took it from a medieval monastery. In the tenth century a famous bishop of Augsburg, St Ulrich, had founded a monastery in that city, dedicated to the saint he revered, a holy woman named Afra. Afra had been martyred when the Emperor Diocletian was persecuting Christians because she had refused to worship him as a god. A former prostitute, she said, 'Let this body which has sinned suffer, but I will not ruin my soul with false worship.' She was carried to an island in the River Lech, not far from Oberammergau, tied to a stake and set alight. Bishop Ulrich's reverence for her led him to spend his last illness lying on the floor among burnt ashes which were formed into the shape of a cross. After his death, his own renown spread and the monastery was jointly dedicated to Ulrich and Afra.

In the fifteenth century the monks there wrote a passion play which, a century later, was revised and improved by a Mastersinger called Sebastian Wild. This was the play borrowed by the people of Oberammergau for their performance in 1634, and again ten years later.

It must have been enjoyable. Just as the minds of most men and women of that time were frequently filled with images of devils (they sometimes even saw them walking about in times of stress, such as the plague years), so their play brought these devils to life. Sebastian Wild added a prologue to the play of the Augsburg monks, urging spectators to treat the proceedings reverently. Immediately a devil came on to the stage and read a letter from Lucifer urging them to treat it with contempt.

But the devil was too serious a figure to be mocked all the time in this play. When Judas is paid his thirty pieces of silver for betraying Jesus, Lucifer's minions dance round as each coin is slowly counted out, reciting a little verse over each one. And at the crucifixion, where Jesus is flanked by two thieves, three devils carry the unconverted thief to hell, while an angel appears to carry the converted one to heaven.

The villagers of Oberammergau at last began to tire of this play. They were committed to their vow, but not to any one drama of the Passion. The text of the original play is still extant, and we can see how they covered with strips of paper passages they had grown to dislike, adding new sentences and bits of dialogue.

But the devils did not disappear from their performances for a long time. One particularly grisly scene used to take place after Judas had

(*top*) Mary in 1880 –
Anastasia Krach; and (*below*)
in 1890 – Ottilie Zwinck

hanged himself. The Oberammergauers would arrange for his entrails to fall out. These were in fact made by the local baker and butcher out of bread and sausages, and a gang of devils would rush in and eat them. Fortunately this scene was eventually cut out.

What does survive from the medieval play is its tender treatment of the biblical characters. The relationship of Jesus and Mary was seen in remarkably human terms, and this feeling can be perceived when the villagers keep their vow today. 'My dearly beloved son,' wept the Virgin Mary over the Saviour's dead body in the old play, 'have I to live now without you? Dead as you are, I shall still love you. All women in the world, join in suffering with me. Help me to mourn my child.'

Just as the villagers turned to the monks of St Ulrich and St Afra to find their first Passion Play after 1633, so later they sought the help of monks to make further changes. Slowly, in a way that is fascinating to chronicle, the Oberammergauers transformed their play from its fairly knockabout medieval origins to today's deeply moving religious drama.

In all this they were able to rely on the unfailing help of the monks of nearby Ettal. Ettal monastery was famous long before the plague came to Oberammergau. The valley in which it stands was ruled in the ninth century by a Guelph named Ethiko (the name 'Ettal' derives from 'Ethiko's Tal' or valley) and from his descendants it eventually passed to the Wittelsbachs who became Dukes of Bavaria.

In the year 1327 one of these, Ludwig of Bavaria, journeyed to Rome. There he vowed to found a monastery on his return, to house twenty monks and an abbot, along with a noble house for thirteen knights and their wives, plus the widows of six other knights. He brought back from Rome a miracle-working statue of the Virgin Mary, which is still at Ettal. It is said that he chose the site for his monastery at a place where his horse suddenly stopped and genuflected.

It was to the monks of this monastery that the villagers of Oberammergau turned for literary advice in the keeping of their vow of 1633. Occasionally, too, they sought the help of the monks of Rottenbuch, a few more miles away, as they rewrote and refined their sacred drama.

At the beginning of the eighteenth century the villagers' tastes were clearly changing. They wanted, it seems, something far more florid than the simple medieval play they had hitherto performed. They also hankered after poetry rather than the simple dialect speech of the mystery plays.

In 1715 the monks of Ettal helped to revise their text to fit in with these wishes. But they did not yet feel they wanted to abandon the devils. In fact a monk of Rottenbuch, Anselm Manhardt, added *more* devils – but this time of a less earthy kind. He gave them allegorical names, such as sin, death, greed and envy. These eighteenth-century monks were much preoccupied with thoughts of hell; in 1740 the prior of Rottenbuch, Clemens Prasser, who had been parish priest at Oberammergau, rewrote several scenes of the Passion Play to emphasize the danger of eternal damnation.

All this tampering with the text resulted in an untidy play with no real unity. For the performance of 1750 the parish priest of Oberammergau

(*top*) Mary in 1900 – Anna Flunger; and (*below*) in 1950 – Annemarie Mayr

decided that the play must be completely rewritten. He called upon Ferdinand Rosner, an extremely talented monk of Ettal, to produce a new version.

By any standards, Rosner's work was brilliant. He created a Passion Play in the style of an Italian opera. His play, almost a thousand lines long, was written in long rhyming couplets set to music, with linking prose dialogue. Ferdinand Rosner kept the allegorical devils – sin, death, greed, envy, and so on – and the swarm of devils who ate Judas's entrails. Some of his stage directions have become famous: to simulate the earthquake at Christ's death, he arranged for one villager to roll a barrel filled with stones, while others shot off guns and filled the stage with smoke.

But nobody liked his play. The performances of 1750 and 1760 were, it was thought, far too burdened with notions of hell, damnation and general gloom. The villagers begged Father Magnus Knipfelberger of Ettal to work over Rosner's text. As Rosner's pupil he could not be expected to discard all of his master's play. He kept about half of it, including the allegorical devils, but he toned down the more flowery passages. This was the text used in 1780, 1790 and the interrupted season of 1800–1801.

Now, however, the Oberammergau Passion Play was under threat from a totally unexpected quarter. The Protestant Reformers did not object to the medieval mystery plays. Martin Luther himself observed that 'Such spectacles often do more good and produce a greater impression than sermons.' But to the so-called 'Enlightenment' of the eighteenth century, the simple, sometimes crude drama of the common people seemed to bring religion into disrepute. As the Prince-Archbishop of Salzburg put it in 1779, 'The mixture of sacred and profane, the ludicrous and disagreeable effect of the bad acting, the intentional buffooneries ... brings scandal on church and religion.'

The secular authorities agreed. On 31 March 1770 the Prince-Elector of Bavaria, Maximilian Joseph, banned all passion plays in his domains, including the Passion Play at Oberammergau. The villagers were deeply disturbed, and twenty of their number were deputed to appeal against the ban. In April 1770 they put forward five arguments in defence of their play:

1. They could not and would not break the solemn vow made by their forefathers in 1633;
2. they had already printed four thousand copies of the text and could not afford to leave them unsold;
3. they had spent 200 florins on repairing the costumes for their coming production and on building a stage;
4. very many persons now came to see the play from villages and towns of Bavaria – amounting to 10,000 people in the season of 1760 – and it was too late to stop them coming now;
5. the Passion Play at Oberammergau could in no wise be considered impious, blasphemous or absurd, since it was supervised both by the local parish priest and the monks of Ettal.

Oberammergau as a tourist centre: the Hotel Wittelsbach retains the charm of the painted houses

These pleas were of no avail. On 2 May the answer came: 'If the play is in accordance with a vow, they shall replace it by some other religious devotion, such as an annual sermon or several hours of prayer.' A further appeal from Oberammergau to the Elector himself was rejected 'once and for ever'.

Now the faithfulness of the village to its vow of 1633 was truly being put to the test. Bravely the Oberammergauers ignored the royal ban. They escaped without punishment.

The next Elector, Karl Theodor, proved more amenable. He wished to restore prosperity to the country. When they appealed to him, the villagers wisely stressed the economic importance of their Passion Play in bringing employment and visitors to the region. On 8 January 1780 Karl Theodor decreed: 'It may be repeated henceforth every ten years and performed in public without any hindrance.'

This was a particular testimony to Oberammergau's persistence in faithfulness to its vow. Karl Theodor did not like passion plays in general. He banned others in Bavaria, sometimes specifically pointing out that this ban did not apply to Oberammergau.

For a time the threat to the play and to the vow came from war. In 1800 the disturbed times allowed the villagers to produce only five performances of their play. They found this was too few to satisfy those who wished to see them as they obeyed their solemn vow, so they gave four more performances in the following year.

And now they found themselves once again at odds with official Bavarian policy. Their play had an enemy in Munich, Count Montgelas,

Visitors enjoy the sun
outside the Alte Post hotel

who in 1810 persuaded the new Elector to threaten a fine of 30 Reichs-talers on Oberammergau if the villagers went ahead with their play. It required another deputation to court to have this threat removed. The Oberammergau play was described as 'a harmless affair . . . more or less a rural festivity'.

By this time the villagers had produced a completely rewritten version. In a paradoxical fashion, the edicts banning passion plays in Bavaria greatly improved the text used at Oberammergau. For the first time the play became almost entirely biblical.

The man responsible was another monk of Ettal named Othmar Weiss. By now the monastery had been officially suppressed as a result of the 'secularization' of 1803. Othmar Weiss alone had lived on there in a monk's cell, before becoming parish priest of Eschenlohe. He therefore knew well the delicacy of the task he was undertaking. Oberammergau needed a passion play that was totally unobjectionable and yet still worthy of the long-held vow.

He based his text almost entirely on Holy Scripture. The one exception to this rule was the story of St Veronica. The legend of the woman who offered her scarf to Jesus so that he could wipe away the sweat and blood from his face as he carried his cross to Calvary is found in its present form only in the fourteenth century. The rest of the story of Jesus's passion as told by Othmar Weiss derives entirely from the New Testament.

Weiss did, however, keep one remarkable dramatic device of Ferdinand Rosner's text. Rosner had introduced into the Oberammergau Passion Play eighteen 'living tableaux'. These were scenes from the Old

The Pre-Raphaelite Mary Magdalene of 1890

Testament, introduced at suitable points in the progress of Jesus's last days on earth. Frequently crowded with actors but entirely motionless, it was as if a living scene had been, for a moment, frozen.

Othmar Weiss was a genius. A doctor of the University of Ingolstadt, he never abandoned his monk's habit even though his community had been driven from Ettal. As well as working as a parish priest, he ran both a brewery and the local Oberammergau school. After Eschenlohe he became parish priest at Unterammergau and then at Jesenwang, where he lived until his death in 1843. And he produced a passion play acceptable to the Bavarian authorities. So successful were the productions of 1811 that further performances were allowed in 1815. Weiss continued to refine the play. He kept some of the old merriment (a visitor of 1820 records that angels appeared and disappeared on 'invisible' wires). The play he wrote is substantially the one still used today. He conceived, for instance, of the idea of Jesus's entry into Jerusalem at the start of the Passion Play as something triumphant rather than furtive or fearful. Weiss's Jesus, riding on a donkey, appears as a king.

The troubles of the Passion Play were over. After 1820 members of the Bavarian royal family became its leading supporters rather than its opponents. One hundred years after the first performance of Othmar Weiss's new text, the grateful citizens of Oberammergau erected a memorial tablet in his honour on the south wall of Jesenwang church. Without him they would undoubtedly have been forced to break their vow.

By a remarkable coincidence, living in Oberammergau when Weiss was rewriting the Passion Play was a gifted musician named Rochus Dedler. Dedler had been born in the village in 1779, the seventh son of an innkeeper (who plied his trade in what is now called the 'Dedler-Haus'). The schoolmaster in the village was Michael Reichard, who had set to music some sacred songs contributed by Father Magnus Knipfelberger to Father Rosner's text. Reichard soon perceived that his pupil Dedler had outstanding ability. He sent the boy as a chorister to the monastery at Rottenbuch, where Dedler proved so proficient both at playing and composing music that when he reached the age of fourteen the monks sent him as a poor scholar to the Gregorian music seminary in Munich.

Dedler's aim was to enter the monastery of Ettal, but 'secularization' made this impossible. He was obliged to earn his living not only as schoolmaster and church organist in Oberammergau (where he had a house provided by the village and a salary of 400 guilders a year) but also as organist and choirmaster both at Ettal and at Rottenbuch. Overwork undoubtedly ruined his health and led to his early death in 1822. Even his work for the Passion Play was dogged by ill-luck. But, helped and inspired by his friend the last prior of Rottenbuch who had settled in Oberammergau after 'secularization', he succeeded in setting to music much of Weiss's text. He composed first for the play of 1811 and rewrote his music to fit in with Weiss's remodelled text of 1815. Then, on the night of 18 November 1817, a fire which destroyed thirty-four houses in Oberammergau took with it all Dedler's belongings, including his precious music. Undeterred, the ailing schoolmaster rewrote his music for the performances of 1820.

On- and off-stage: (*top*)
Gabriele Gropper playing
Mary Magdalene in the
production of 1950, and
(*below*) in her parents' shop

Dedler was greatly influenced by Mozart and by the baroque music of the eighteenth century. For many years his work for the Oberammergau Passion Play was underestimated. After the 1890 Oberammergau season, Dean F.W. Farrar of St Paul's wrote that his music 'contains none of those infinitely pathetic movements and crashing outbursts with which the genius of Handel has made the world familiar, nor has it the marvellously inwoven harmonies of the Passion Music of [Johann] Sebastian Bach, yet it is throughout admirably suited to its purpose'. Today we have a better estimate of the value of Dedler's kind of music. Dedler was paid precious little for it at the time; in 1815 the villagers paid him fifty-three florins – less than it cost to construct the Passion Play stage for that year! In 1949 the village commissioned Eugen Pabst, the Oberammergau-born director of the Cologne male-voice choir (and a friend of Richard Strauss – Pabst conducted Strauss's *Death and Transfiguration* at the great composer's funeral), to produce a worthy edition of Dedler's Passion Play music. This is the version used at Oberammergau today.

The villagers, in faithfulness to their vow, had created a unique Passion Play. Moreover it had been created almost entirely in the Ammer valley. In the mid nineteenth century it was to be revised again by one of Oberammergau's greatest adopted sons, its parish priest Alois Daisenberger.

Daisenberger had been born in nearby Oberau in 1799. His schoolmaster was Othmar Weiss. After further study at the University of Landshut he was ordained in 1822. But he remained much loved in the valley where he was born, and when the living of Oberammergau became vacant in 1845 the villagers petitioned the royal authorities to make Alois Daisenberger their parish priest because, they wrote, 'he was born near here, at Oberau, and totally understands our needs'. The authorities agreed, and Daisenberger stayed in Oberammergau for the rest of his long life, resolutely turning down many offers of preferment to more exalted positions.

In 1850 the villagers asked him to revise the text of their Passion Play. Daisenberger remained extremely faithful to the work of his teacher Othmar Weiss, but he did shorten the play a little, cutting down over-long speeches, removing a good number of outdated words and some colloquialisms and omitting a few passages that he considered redundant. He had far too much respect for the work of Rochus Dedler to touch any of the sacred songs.

This was the play that Eduard Devrient saw in 1850 and so much revered. 'One sees that the performance is not learned,' he wrote; 'it is lived.' And he added: 'One cannot say too much about this highly remarkable drama of the people, in order to spread a thorough knowledge and a just appreciation of its beauty and sublimity.'

Devrient's praise brought many people to see the Passion Play at Oberammergau. Some came to criticize. Humbly, Daisenberger noted their criticisms and wherever he thought them justified, he would revise his text. His Jesus – inherited from Othmar Weiss – is an intensely human figure. Daisenberger was conscious that Oberammergau now had a new international responsibility to present a worthy account of the Passion of its Saviour in accordance with the two-hundred-year-old vow;

Interrupted in 1870 by the Franco-Prussian War, performances were resumed the following year. In 1871 the Passion Play was seen by the Prince and Princess of Wales, travelling incognito

but he never lost his humility. He worked, he said, 'for the love of my divine Redeemer and the edification of the Christian world'. At the same time he insisted that the Oberammergau Passion Play was something utterly unpretentious. 'It is not our aim to shine in the art of acting,' he said when preaching on Whit Sunday, 1870. 'That would be presumptuous and ridiculous in simple country people. But it must be the earnest desire of each one of us to try to represent worthily this most holy mystery.'

In 1633 the villagers of Oberammergau could have in no way forecast one paradoxical blessing from their vow. Two and a half centuries later this vow, made as a result of a plague caused by bitter religious wars, could bring together men and women of very different kinds; Catholic and Protestant, believer and unbeliever. The celebrated English critic Matthew Arnold observed that the performances of 1871 united people 'who once seemed as far as the poles asunder'.

Nor could the villagers of 1633 have realized that their successors, in utterly committed faithfulness to the vow, would create what Matthew Arnold perceived to be a unique religious masterpiece. Arnold was no woolly-minded literary critic, and he pointed out that the performances of the Passion Play provoked in the audiences genuine transports of pity, love and gratitude. 'To find anyone who has seen the play and not been deeply interested and moved by it, is very rare,' he judged. 'The peasants of the neighbouring country, the great and fashionable world, the ordinary tourist, were all at Ammergau, and were delighted.' Over a hundred years later that judgement still holds good.

3 A Play for All Time

'They now remove the rope from Christ's feet and bind him with strips of linen round his body, hands and arms as well as round his breast and loins, so that he will not fall from the cross should he become unconscious.'

So runs a stage direction for taking the body of Jesus down from the cross in the version of the Oberammergau Passion Play written by Othmar Weiss in 1815. Such care is still needed today. The actors playing Christ must grasp the nails of the great Oberammergau cross with their hands and balance on the tiny sloping platform with their feet for twenty-eight minutes. It is dangerous and taxing work. Flesh-coloured bandages round the actors' wrists help a little. But a great deal still depends on the stamina of the man playing Jesus. Rudolf Zwink took the role as a very young man in 1980. It was therefore possible to re-elect him to play Jesus for the special performances of 1984. But Gregor Breitsamter, who also played Jesus in 1980, was in his late forties when the time came for the 1984 re-election. Physically he could not have taken the part for a second season. He was offered and accepted a role in the chorus.

Successive seasons of the Passion Play since it was rewritten by Othmar Weiss in 1811 have thus thrown up the same problems and these problems have been dealt with in traditional ways. This accounts for much of the artistic success of the plays over the last hundred years and more. Actors have always relied on tradition. The great English Shakespearean actor, Henry Irving, for instance, sought out the old player who as Polonius had played opposite Kean's Hamlet. Irving closely questioned him about Kean's performance, especially about what he had done in his famous closet scene, and then reinterpreted Kean's performance in his own fashion. So the actors and directors of the Oberammergau Passion Play both build and rely on the interpretations of predecessors. The play as seen today has been formed over many generations.

Virtually the whole village knows it by heart. In recent years the village has at times been called on to decide whether or not the play should be changed. Those who may be offered leading parts will almost certainly have played smaller roles in the past. Anton Preisinger, who played Jesus in both 1950 and 1960, had played an angel at the age of ten in 1922 and Lazarus in 1934. His sister had taken the part of Mary Magdalene in 1930. The 'prologue' of 1950, Alois Lang, had played Jesus in 1930 and 1934. Melchior Breitsamter played Pontius Pilate in all three productions of 1930, 1934 and 1950. This was no new phenomenon. The actor playing St Peter in 1890 had done so for four seasons, as had the actor playing Caiaphas the high priest. Others had played various roles over several seasons. The ageing Gregor Lechner, who took the part of Simon of

Bethany in 1890, had played Judas in the 1870–71 season and in 1880. Johann Zwink, who played Judas in 1890, had carefully watched Lechner's performances of previous years.

The first photographs of the Oberammergau Passion Play were taken by Ludwig II's court photographer in 1871. A comparison of these with both the engravings with which Eduard Devrient illustrated his famous account of the 1850 season and with later photographs reveals how closely performances over the years resemble each other. And this remains especially true of the 'living tableaux'.

Here the producer must often deploy over a hundred actors, ranging from leading characters of the Old Testament to children and spectators. Indeed, to make their proper dramatic impact these tableaux must be immediately recognizable and also strikingly powerful in their conception.

The way Ferdinand Rosner, who first introduced the Old Testament tableaux into the Oberammergau Passion Play, understood the relationship between Old and New Testaments is not shared by the twentieth-century Christian for the most part. Briefly, Rosner (following a very long Christian tradition which can be seen elsewhere – in, for instance, Handel's 'Messiah') regarded the Old Testament not just as a prelude to the New but in many ways foreshadowing it. The deeds and stories of the ancient Hebrews were, he supposed, paralleled by the events recounted in the New Testament. The eye of faith could see that what

The mid-eighteenth-century onion-domed tower of Oberammergau parish church rises above a picturesque street

happened before the birth of Jesus reflected in a miraculous manner the events of his lifetime. What we might see merely as striking coincidences, Rosner and Othmar Weiss perceived as deliberate similarities inspired by God in sacred history. Once this is understood, the relationship between the 'living tableaux' taken from the Old Testament and the life of Jesus becomes dramatically extremely effective.

The first of the 'living tableaux', the expulsion of Adam and Eve from the Garden of Eden, perfectly introduces the notion that the passion and death of Jesus which we are about to see is the divine means of dealing with human sin and our fall from grace. Thenceforth the tableaux and their relationship with the New Testament events become visually striking and at the same time more artificial. The Passion Play presents the story of Tobias leaving home (taken from the book of Tobit) as a parallel to the scene where Jesus takes his final leave of his mother before journeying to Jerusalem and to his death.

Then a 'living tableau' illustrates the passage from the Song of Songs in which a bride laments the departure of her bridegroom. 'I opened to my beloved; but my beloved had withdrawn himself and was gone. I sought him but I could not find him. I called to him but he gave me no answer.' This beautiful and moving passage is seen as an image of the grief of the Virgin Mary after Jesus has gone.

Less obvious is the significance of the 'living tableau' illustrating a story from the book of Esther. King Ahasuerus, says the book, 'loved

The interior of the rococo parish church, designed by Joseph Schmuzer in 1736. The high altar, finished in 1762, and the side altars were created by the famous Franz Xavier Schmädl

The magnificent Moses in
the production of 1890

Esther above all women and she obtained grace and favour in his sight
more than all the virgins, so that he set the royal crown upon her head
and made her queen instead of Vashti'. In the Oberammergau play this
comes to signify the rejection by God of those who do not acknowledge
Jesus as the messiah.

Other tableaux correspond to the events of the New Testament more
directly. The scenes in which God gives manna to the children of Israel
in the desert, and in which Moses' emissaries into Canaan return with a
cluster of grapes, are related in the play to the Last Supper, when Jesus
gives his disciples heavenly food in the form of bread and wine. And
when the brothers of the young Joseph sell him to the Ishmaelites for
twenty pieces of silver, it is easy to make a comparison with Judas
betraying his Lord for a similar reward. In connection with Judas, the
play also exploits dramatically a yet more remarkable coincidence between Old and New Testaments. According to the Second book of
Samuel, the warrior Joab decided to kill a man named Amasa. They met
near Gibeon. 'And Joab said to Amasa, "Is it well with thee, my brother?" And Joab took Amasa by the beard with his right hand to kiss
him. But Amasa took no heed of the sword that was in Joab's hand. So
Joab smote him therewith in the belly and shed out his bowels to the
ground and struck him not again. And he died.' The New Testament
parallel to this bloodthirsty scene is the moment when Judas betrays
Jesus to his enemies by kissing him.

Because of the theatrical power of the play, what might seem laboured
correspondences do have a telling impact. The play seeks parallels to the
mockery of Jesus's trials in Old Testament episodes. Jesus before Annas
is hit in the face. The corresponding 'living tableau' is the story of the
prophet Micah, who speaks the truth to the rulers of Israel and Judah
and for his pains is struck in the face by a sycophantic courtier. The false
witnesses at Jesus's trial before Caiaphas are paralleled by those who lie
about innocent Naboth before King Ahab. And the ridicule heaped on
Jesus by Herod enables the producer of the play to present in tableau
form the moment when Samson, ridiculed by the Philistines, pulls down
their pagan temple on their heads.

Clearly some of these parallels are laboured. Adam, bitterly eating
bread after his expulsion from the Garden of Eden, is fairly remote from
the bitter trials and passion of Jesus. Joseph presented by Pharaoh to the
Egyptians is scarcely a counterpart to Jesus presented to the people by
Pontius Pilate. But other Old Testament references in the play – such as
the 'living tableaux' depicting a scapegoat and the ram which Abraham
sacrificed instead of his son Isaac – do reasonably reflect the sacrifice of
Jesus's life on the cross.

To find the resurrection of Jesus foreshadowed in the Old Testament
has taxed the ingenuity of Christian scholars for many centuries. The
Oberammergau Passion Play follows tradition by utilizing the scenes of
the children of Israel crossing the Red Sea and Jonah being vomited out
of the whale. To some of us in the twentieth century the correspondences
may again seem far-fetched; but the play cannot be faulted for taking up
longstanding Christian interpretations of the Old Testament.

And two other considerations apply here. First, New Testament writers themselves give a lead in treating the Old Testament in this fashion. To give one example used at Oberammergau: Moses, it is said, lifted up a bronze serpent in the wilderness; it healed the children of Israel of snake bites; St John's Gospel tells us that Jesus declared that 'as Moses lifted up the serpent in the wilderness, even so must the Son of man be lifted up, that whosoever believes may in him have eternal life'. In using the story of Moses' serpent as a 'living tableau', the Oberammergau play is simply following the lead of St John. Secondly, the use of 'living tableaux' from the Old Testament to emphasize aspects of the New can be justified simply because, dramatically, it works.

Oberammergau's Passion Play is effective partly because it draws on so many different elements in the Christian heritage. Many of the tableaux, as well as some of the scenes of Christ's passion, have an added impact because they deliberately reflect great works of art. The descent from the cross mirrors Rubens, whose painting of the subject was found reproduced in many a Bavarian inn in the nineteenth century. The moment when Jesus is presented by Pilate to the people draws on Correggio's 'Ecce Homo'. The Last Supper draws inspiration from Leonardo da Vinci, even to the details of the table and stools.

What is remarkable is the way diverse elements have been blended into a deeply satisfying whole. The Passion Play at Oberammergau as we know it today harmoniously combines elements from four different traditions in our culture. First, of course, it celebrates the Jewish and Christian religious tradition. But this is combined with a dramatic device drawn from the Greeks, namely the 'prologue' and chorus commenting on scenes as they are revealed. Thirdly, it is enhanced by the great baroque musical tradition. Lastly, it embodies the genius of these Bavarian villagers. And it is a living culture. The Passion Play will change as the living tradition of Oberammergau continues to develop.

Throughout, the aim remains absolutely clear: to depict and illuminate the passion, death and resurrection of Jesus in accordance with the vow of 1633. This provided the driving force of Othmar Weiss's text, which had no fewer than eighty scenes. In cutting down this text by one quarter, Alois Daisenberger intensified that urgency and drive.

'The crucifixion must be *pictured*,' insisted the distinguished American New Testament scholar, John Knox. 'Men must see it and feel it, imaginatively entering into the sufferings of Christ and sensing the awful significance of what happened on Calvary. The story of the Passion must be told in such a fashion that the stark reality of it be felt and the full redemptive meaning of it be realized.' This is precisely what the Passion Play at Oberammergau sets out to achieve.

The story of Christ's passion is one of human fickleness, of triumph and despair, of nobility and courage and of unfaithful friends. It involves an unjust charge and unjust trial, as well as a totally undeserved and cruel death. It can be seen both as a human tragedy and as a deeply theological and spiritual event of immense significance for the whole of mankind. This is what the inhabitants of one small Bavarian village have been attempting to portray for over three hundred and fifty years.

(*top*) St John in 1890, and (*below*) in 1950

(*top*) Caiaphas in 1890, and (*below*) in 1950

The story opens with Jesus riding in triumph into Jerusalem, but seated not on a charger, but on a humble donkey. At Oberammergau this scene takes place in the early morning, with a huge crowd of villagers, including children, deployed on the stage, surrounding Jesus until he rides out from them as they wave their palms of welcome. Here Jesus was consciously taking as his model a sentence from the Old Testament prophet Zechariah: 'Rejoice greatly, O daughter of Zion; shout, O daughter of Jerusalem, behold your king comes unto you. He is just and brings salvation, lowly and riding on an ass.' As the British scholar H.E.W. Turner once observed, 'He comes a lowly King; they greet Him with cries more appropriate to a conquering hero. Nobody appeared to notice a figure which to Jesus was of the essence of the scene – the ass itself.'

In the Passion Play written by Othmar Weiss and adapted by Alois Daisenberger, Jesus next went to the Temple. There he drove out those who made a living from selling doves and changing money. As a result these traders so hated him that they hurried to the Jewish leaders to persuade them to turn against Jesus and seek out the follower who was to betray him, Judas. Now this version of the events is not quite true to the Gospel record. Three of the four Gospels certainly portray Jesus as overthrowing the tables of the money-changers and the seats of those who sold doves, at this point in his earthly life – St John's Gospel puts the episode at the start of Jesus's ministry. But Weiss and Daisenberger took a dramatic liberty with the evidence of the Gospels in making these men vindictive enemies of Jesus because he threatened their livelihood. The Gospels make it clear that Judas approached Jesus's enemies of his own accord, offering to betray his master. The traders of the Temple had nothing further to do with it. Today the Oberammergau story (for reasons we shall examine in more detail later) has been brought into line with the biblical witness. But Jesus still attacks those who, as he put it, were transforming his Father's house from a house of prayer to a den of thieves. To quote Elizabethe Corathiel's description of the Passion Play as she saw it in both 1934 and 1950, 'Tables are overthrown; money rolls away. With a whirring of wings, a cloud of doves, released from upturned cages, ascends towards the blue sky.'

After these stirring scenes, the progress of Jesus towards his inevitable death becomes calmer, more domestic. Caiaphas, who was High Priest for that year, fearful of the effect Jesus might have on the occupying Roman forces, declares that it is better for one man to die in order to save all the rest. Jesus dines in the house of Simon of Bethany, and there a woman anoints him with precious ointment. Traditionally this woman has been identified as Mary Magdalene, as she is in the Oberammergau portrayal of the incident. It is as if she is anointing his body as women of her time used to do before a burial.

Here again the dangerous character of Judas is revealed, as he publicly attacks the notion of wasting such a precious ointment on Jesus. Here, too, Jesus's mother makes her first appearance in the Passion Play, to take her last farewell of her son.

Jesus now arranges for his Last Supper with his disciples. On the way to Jerusalem, the city for which he weeps, he is still at odds with Judas, who now agrees to betray Jesus to his enemies. For this reason, when he hears Jesus at the Last Supper foretell that one of his followers will betray him, Judas slips away. The Last Supper itself, though faithful to the text of the Gospels (which are in fact not entirely harmonious here), is not shown at Oberammergau as it would have taken place in the Jerusalem of Jesus's day. Then, for example, those taking part would certainly have been reclining instead of sitting. At Oberammergau, under the powerful influence of Leonardo da Vinci's famous painting of the event, they sit on stools at a table.

Events now move swiftly. Judas is bought by Jesus's enemies for thirty pieces of silver. Jesus first prays in agony in the Garden of Gethsemane, his followers unable to stay awake long enough to comfort him. Then Judas betrays him to an armed band by kissing him. Jesus surrenders, refusing to let his followers defend him by force of arms, and the first half of the Passion Play ends.

The second act deals with the public trials and humiliations of Jesus. He is tried not only before two of his Jewish enemies, Annas and Caiaphas, but is also sent to King Herod and brought before the Roman procurator, Pontius Pilate. This complex way of condemning an innocent man has its roots in the historical realities of Jerusalem in the first century of the Christian era. Almost certainly the High Priest Caiaphas was not recognized as having any spiritual authority by the Jewish Sanhedrin, the council of rabbis which strove to preserve the traditions of Judaism during the difficult years of Roman domination. Whereas Caiaphas and

The crucifixion in the production of 1850

Annas represent the party that collaborated with the Roman powers, the Sanhedrin tried to preserve some independence. It is interesting that, according to the Acts of the Apostles, both St Peter and St Paul are saved from the enmity of the High Priest by the Sanhedrin. But in the case of Jesus, the High Priest and his party win the day.

But Jesus was crucified, and the Jewish leaders of his day had no power or right to crucify anyone. Crucifixion was a penalty inflicted by the Romans to bring slaves to heel, and those who might rebel against the Roman power.

Who, then, was responsible for the death of Jesus? It is impossible to say, and the Oberammergau Passion Play reflects this uncertainty. Jesus is passed on from Annas to Caiaphas and from Caiaphas to Pontius Pilate. Pilate learns that he comes from Galilee and therefore sends him to be judged by Herod Antipas, who rules there. Jesus himself had referred to Herod as 'that fox'. But Herod refuses either to fall in with the wishes of Annas and Caiaphas, or to do Pilate's work for him. Jesus is sent back to the procurator, who then appeals to the crowd. Will they choose for release Jesus or a known criminal named Barabbas? Most of the crowd shout for Barabbas.

For centuries, in answer to the question: Who was responsible for the death of Jesus? the Church answered, the Jews. As Professor C.K. Barrett has written, 'in that belief Christians have, from time to time, committed crimes against the Jewish people of which Christians today ought to be - and, I believe, are - ashamed. The record is a sorry one, and nothing can excuse it. Jesus himself did not encourage us to take vengeance: if anyone strikes you on one cheek, let him have the other one too.' According to this teaching of Jesus himself, anti-Semitism would be wrong even if it were possible to say that the Jews ultimately crucified him. But the Gospel record here is one of confusion. And the people of Oberammergau, clearly acknowledging this, today represent this confusion in their Passion Play.

In all his trials, Jesus is beaten and spat upon. The play, following the Gospels, makes it clear that he is innocent both of the charge of blaspheming against God and of fostering rebellion against the Romans. Judas, bitterly ashamed at what he has done, attempts to return the thirty pieces of silver to those who bought him, and then hangs himself. Jesus's companion Peter betrays his master, as Jesus foretold at the Last Supper.

So the Passion Play moves to the crucifixion and death of Jesus. The choir which has been commenting on these events is now dressed in black. Jesus drags his cross to Calvary, where he is crucified between two thieves. In the past this scene was more gruesomely presented than it is nowadays. There is at Oberammergau today no excessively realistic attempt to depict the nailing of Jesus to the cross. The two thieves between whom he is crucified are already raised on their crosses when the curtain opens. Jesus on his great cross is slowly raised upright.

No one Gospel agrees with the others about what Jesus said from the cross. Altogether they record seven different utterances, each one profoundly moving. Christians in the past have been accustomed to setting together these utterances as the seven words from the cross, and the

(*above*) Melchior
Breitsamter, playing Pontius
Pilate, washes his hands in
the 1950 production

(*top left*) Jakob Klucker
playing Annas in 1950;
(*below left*) Heinrich
Zunterer playing Herod in
1950

Oberammergau play does so too. Then Jesus dies. His side is pierced by a spear. He is taken from the cross and placed in the lap of his mother, in preparation for his burial.

What happened then? The Bible does not say that Jesus rose from the dead. What it says is that God raised him from the dead. Here is something that transcends history. History cannot depict an act of God so as to make him visible. The play ends by showing two final scenes, the resurrection and the ascension of Jesus. The latter is depicted as a 'living tableau'. And neither has been judged as entirely satisfactory. It is possible to *proclaim* Jesus's resurrection. It is scarcely possible to depict it. Equally, Christ's ascension is, in the Bible, couched in mythical and symbolic language; any attempt to show what might have actually happened would be bound to fail.

For this reason the shrewd American who visited Oberammergau in 1910 spoke for many when he suggested that just as in the past scenes have been cut from the Passion Play, 'Time may bring one or two further omissions – the disappearance of the figure springing rapidly from the grave on Easter morning and the final and of necessity ineffective tableau of Christ-in-glory.' Montrose J. Moses suggested that simply showing Jesus's empty tomb, or perhaps his risen appearance to Mary, would be enough.

To depict the resurrection may still be a problem for the villagers of Oberammergau. It is worth insisting that for those who three hundred and fifty years ago made the vow that they would henceforth try to depict it, the resurrection was not a *problem*, but the *solution* to their problems – to the problem of their grief for those of their village who had failed to survive the plague and to their own hopes and deepest desires for a risen life.

Properly to portray the passion of Jesus takes time, and the Oberammergau play combines the passion with scenes from the Old Testament and with the interventions of the chorus. Even today, when the play has been considerably shortened, performances begin at nine o'clock in the morning and continue until half-past five in the afternoon, with a break of three hours in the middle.

For the audience it scarcely seems long enough. For the principal actors, each performance is an enormous strain. It seems extraordinary that 1980 was the first season in which two actors played alternate performances in the principal parts. (Children's roles have been played in relays of four for much longer.)

The seats of the Oberammergau theatre are not over-upholstered; if they were, the perfect acoustics of the theatre would be ruined. Yet again and again visitors testify that they hardly notice the time pass, such is the pace of the performance. But at the end, while the audience is exhilarated, the actors are exhausted.

Performances of such intensity have reconciled to the Passion Play many who were initially opposed to it. The British, for instance, have sometimes displayed a lingering puritanism which objected to seeing Jesus depicted on the stage. In 1890 Dean Farrar observed that: 'There are not a few English men and women, of earnest and reverent minds, who denounce the play as blasphemous, and consider it a sin to witness it.' Farrar himself considered such an opinion as 'harsh and insular'. In any case, such people were a dying breed at the time he wrote. The Passion Play soon won over even the most puritanical. As Dean Stanley wrote in 1860, it made the Gospel stories real. It also brought them into the harsh world. Oberammergau showed, he wrote, how 'the hard realities and brutalities of life must, on this occasion, as always, have come

The fashionable world and Bavarian villagers jostle each other, talk and read their scripts at a Passion Play performance in 1860. Jesus carries his cross towards Golgotha. The orchestra director vigorously conducts his fellow-musicians

into contact with the holiest and tenderest of objects, which, by a stretch of the imagination, we usually contrive to keep apart from them'. The villagers of Oberammergau were not seeking to present some child's fairy-tale. And a hundred years after Stanley made his comment, the tourist manager of Oberammergau could observe with satisfaction that ever since Thomas Cook started his first tours to the Bavarian village during Passion Play seasons, the British have been in an overwhelming majority among foreign guests.

This, too, in spite of two world wars with Germany and Britain on opposite sides. The villagers of Oberammergau have had long experience of the struggle to fulfil their vow in the face of war. The first two performances took place during the horrors of the Thirty Years' War. In 1800 Oberammergau managed to put on its play even though over a thousand Frenchmen had occupied the village after bombarding it with artillery. The Franco-Prussian War of 1870 interrupted, but did not stop, the play. After the First World War Germany was exhausted, but the Passion Play season was merely postponed for two years. The Second World War, however, put an end to any production in 1940. The village soon housed a Messerschmitt factory. Armaments were made in the wood-carving schools and artificial limbs in the theatre dressing-rooms.

Ten years later the popularity of Oberammergau had increased remarkably with the coming of group travel. On the left of the engraving a journalist reviews the scene

In spite of the post-war devastation, the Burgermeister of Oberammergau, Raimund Lang, was determined that the vow should again be fulfilled in 1950. The story of that struggle against enormous difficulties – with soldiers billeted in the village and many houses in disrepair – comes later in this book. Suffice it to say that with a loan of one million marks from the Bavarian government the theatre was repaired, roads and water supply were put right, and costumes repaired or replaced.

The Oberammergau Passion Play was produced again in the season of 1950. Raimund Lang's deputy-Burgermeister, Benedikt Stükhl, played Simon of Bethany. His son Benedikt played Caiaphas.

The Second World War had another profound impact on the Oberammergau Passion Play, though one that took time to be worked out properly. The Nazi treatment of the Jews horrified the civilized world. And Christians began, when the war was over, to ask themselves how far their own barely conscious anti-Semitism might have contributed in some way to the Holocaust. The question of assigning blame for the crucifixion of Jesus was now seen to be deeply important. The way in which Jews were portrayed in Christian drama could profoundly affect the way Christians behaved towards Jews in real life. As we shall see, the villagers of Oberammergau did not shirk these questions.

4 Representing the Jews

How realistic can or should a re-enactment of the sufferings of Jesus be? In the late nineteenth century the sensitive Dean Farrar found the realism of the crucifixion scene almost unbearable. A device in the head of the spear that supposedly pierced Christ's side as he hung on the cross left the semblance of a huge bloody gash on the actor's breast. Dean Farrar wondered if 'this scene was not far too majestically sacred for such representations'.

The Oberammergauers themselves were sensitive about such points, too. Throughout the nineteenth century they refined their Passion Play, cutting out any crudely representational portrayal – of, for example, the agony of Jesus in the garden of Gethsemane when, as he prayed (according to St Luke's Gospel), 'his sweat was as it were great drops of blood falling down to the ground'.

Othmar Weiss and Alois Daisenberger had, in their version of the play, taken care to eliminate much of the knockabout fun that actors would wring from their portrayal of devils in previous plays. For a time some of this seems to have survived in the way producers of the Passion Play dealt with Judas, and particularly his spectacular suicide. It was the custom for Judas to conceal under his cloak a black bird – a raven, if possible – to represent his black soul. At his suicide, he would release the bird, which flapped away, obviously to hell. Gradually this element was also dropped. In 1850 at his suicide he climbed the tree before hanging himself, the curtain fell and his death shriek was heard. Ten years later the death shriek was omitted. In 1890 he no longer climbed the tree. 'We see the ragged, wind-swept tree of the field of blood, and we see Judas tear off his girdle,' recorded Dean Farrar, 'but before the actual suicide the curtain falls.'

The only incongruity noted by Farrar at this point was the derisive laughter of the audience after the traitor's death, in contrast with their devout silence at other moments during the play. This derisive laughter was apparently a traditional feature, for Dean Stanley had observed it in 1860. Today that too has disappeared. Even so, Judas still provokes the wrath of some members of the audience. In 1922 one spectator tried to shoot the actor playing Judas. And a guide to the Passion Play theatre assured me that during the 1980 season an irate English lady sought out one of the two Judases of that year and indignantly belaboured him with her umbrella!

To ask how Judas was traditionally portrayed in the Oberammergau play has more than a historical importance. The attitude of Christianity to those who helped to crucify Jesus in part conditioned the way Christians in the past regarded the whole Jewish people. Some Christian believers – failing to see, for instance, that Jesus's entire life was spent among Jews, that he was not only a Jew himself but also found his followers among them, and that as a result those he castigated and those he praised were in both cases almost always from his own people – have made the deeply unfortunate assumption that Jesus's crucifixion somehow uniquely indicted his own people.

Dean Stanley allowed himself the observation in 1860 that the greed of Judas was 'truly Oriental' – as if that particular vice were not shared by the western world as well. Thirty years later Dean Farrar came away with a different impression. He too believed that greed had played its part in the betrayal of Jesus; but the Oberammergau play still left him with the feeling that there might be 'some gleams of hope even in the degradation of Judas'.

Every good drama needs its villains as well as its heroes. To exhibit in the traitor Judas some redeeming features reveals considerable subtlety in the Oberammergau actors and producers. Much more venom seems to have been put into the portrayal of the Jewish Sanhedrin which, observed Stanley, presented '(unintentionally it may be, but, if so, the more impressively) the appearance of a hideous caricature of a great ecclesiastical assembly'. And Dean Farrar, describing the leading priest Nathaniel as played by Sebastian Lang in 1890, said, 'We see in him a picture of the most repulsive features of priestcraft.' To depict on stage a leading opponent of Jesus as coarsely repulsive might be legitimate theatre. It also marks a departure from the ambition to remain faithful to the record of the Bible which both Othmar Weiss and Alois Daisenberger hoped to achieve in their revisions of the play earlier in the nineteenth century.

And in one further particular the Passion Play representation of its villains in 1890 sharply conflicts with the way modern scholars understand the character and achievements of some of Jesus's contemporaries. According to Dean Farrar's recollections, 'The Jewish priests and Pharisees are rightly exhibited to us as so hypocritical as not even to suspect their own hypocrisy.' Now it is true that in parts of the Gospel record Jesus himself is depicted as accusing Pharisees (and others) of hypocrisy. But to assume from this that hypocrisy was the chief characteristic of this particular Jewish sect greatly maligns a group of devout reformers, many of whom longed for a closer walk with God.

That two sensitive and cultivated Englishmen took all this in their stride (so that F. W. Farrar judged the priests and Pharisees to have been 'rightly' exhibited as hypocrites in 1890) shows that the way the Oberammergau play depicted its villains in the nineteenth century was entirely · in accordance with common Christian attitudes. Such attitudes became far more dangerous with the coming to power of Adolf Hitler. They all too easily played into the hands of the virulent anti-Semitism which he fostered.

Hitler himself hypocritically pretended to be deeply committed to Christianity. Privately he hinted that one day he would destroy it. 'I need Bavarian Catholics and Prussian Protestants to make a great Germany,' he said. 'The rest comes later.' Initially, however, his rise to power seemed to inaugurate a spiritual revival in Germany after the 'atheist' Weimar Republic. He claimed to have saved Germany from godless Bolshevism. He promised to restore the German race to its once proud position after the humiliations of the First World War and the punitive Treaty of Versailles.

The community of Oberammergau shared the hopes of most other Germans in the new regime. 1934 marked the tercentenary of the first performance of their Passion Play after the plague years. The official preface to the Jubilee text of the play expressed the new spirit which Hitler seemed to have brought to Germany:

> Time passed on and, after dreadful misery, saved the German people and its tribes from Bolshevism, this pestilence of abandonment of the race created by God. Instead of imminent ruin, we experienced the fortune of a new life which unites us all in our race. Is there any other time more favourable than these days of the suppression of the anti-Christian powers in our fatherland to remember the price the Son of God himself paid for his people, the people who adhere to him and to his banner? Does there exist any greater cause to perform the Holy Play entrusted to our community of Oberammergau than to perform it in this year 1934 as a prayer of thanksgiving with special reverence and solemnity?

The Oberammergauers treated Adolf Hitler as they had treated their former patron Ludwig II of Bavaria. They sent him a special set of mounted photographs of the play and players (now in the Hitler Collection of the United States Library of Congress), inscribed: 'To our Führer, the protector of the cultural treasures of Germany, from the Passion village of Oberammergau.' Many of Hitler's Christian followers believed it was time to stress Jesus's heroic character instead of his resignation and meekness. Until this moment the Jesus portrayed in the Passion Play had for the most part exhibited these last two virtues. Thomas Cook's *American Traveller's Gazette* of 1934 announced that Alois Lang's 'conception of a vigorous fighting Christ was new for Oberammergau'.

Hitler came to the village in 1934 and professed himself pleased with the Passion Play. Some years later, in his table talk of 5 July 1942, he is said to have observed that the play 'convincingly portrayed the menace of Judaism', whereas Pontius Pilate appeared as 'a Roman so racially and intellectually superior that he stands out like a firm clean rock'.

When the full extent of the Nazi treatment of the Jews became clear, the question of this alleged anti-Semitism in the Passion Play was inevitably and rightly raised. Unfortunately, some who should have known better jumped to hasty conclusions before properly examining the evidence. Professor Richard V. Pierard, for instance, wrote in *The New International Dictionary of the Christian Church* that the Passion Play 'was rewritten for the tricentennial performance in 1934 to make Jesus and the disciples appear as Aryan heroes'. This statement is completely untrue. The play of 1934, far from having been rewritten, was virtually the same text as that of 1890.

Even Adolf Hitler's alleged table talk in 1942 cannot be taken at its face value. The Passion Play of 1934 was deemed much less anti-Semitic than the Nazis wanted. When plans for the (abandoned) season of 1940 were mooted, the Nazis decided to commission an entirely new text to fit in with their racialist prejudices.

One person who did try to check the allegations of complicity with Nazi ideals was an Anglo-German expert on the Oberammergau Passion Play, Elizabethe H.C. Corathiel. In 1938 she was commissioned by sections of the British press to investigate rumours that Anton Lang was in trouble with the Nazi authorities for opposing their attempts to interfere in the next production. 'From the very first he seemed to recognize the danger to which religious liberty would be exposed [by National Socialism],' she wrote, 'and, unlike many of his more up-and-coming young colleagues, he decided to remain aloof from the spreading infection of the New Order. It was a dangerous decision, and soon produced disturbing consequences.'

When Elizabethe Corathiel reached Oberammergau in 1938, Anton Lang had just left hospital after a serious operation. He was extremely anxious to deny that anything was wrong between himself and the German state, pointing out that it might be extremely dangerous for him if such rumours were allowed to persist. 'At the time I really could not understand what all the fuss was about – I had no idea of the persecution which was already beginning,' Elizabethe Corathiel reported; 'all I could see was that Anton Lang was a desperately frightened man, and I put it down to his not having yet quite recovered from the operation.' She added: 'Two weeks later, he was dead, and I am now convinced that the political trend at the time hastened his end.'

The man who played Jesus in 1900, 1910 and 1922 was thus a kind of martyr on behalf of the integrity of Oberammergau. Nevertheless, in spite of Lang's probity, the question of anti-Semitism in the text of the Passion Play – however unconscious this once might have been – could not be ignored after the Holocaust of the Second World War. A fresh impetus to reconsider the whole question came from the Christian side, from the second Vatican Council inaugurated by Pope John XXIII. In 1965 the Council called upon Christians to show a new and positive attitude towards Jews. The Council decreed that it was wrong to put the blame for Christ's crucifixion on all the Jews of his time, and that such blame could certainly not be imputed to Jews living today.

The community of Oberammergau asked Father Stephen Schaller, head of the school attached to Ettal monastery, to help them to revise their text, if possible putting it into modern German and certainly excising any anti-Semitic elements. Clearly this involved removing from Daisenberger's text descriptions of Jesus's Jewish enemies as a 'brood of murderers' and a 'gang of wicked men'.

But Schaller went further than this, and his proposals were not acceptable to the Oberammergau community. Basically he wanted them to abandon altogether their nineteenth-century text and return to that created by Father Ferdinand Rosner in 1750.

Rosner's play puts the blame for the crucifixion not on the Jews but on human frailty in general, on jealousy and self-seeking. But the objections to it made by the Oberammergauers were perfectly reasonable. In the first place, Rosner's Passion Play, they said, was extremely boring. 'What we want is theatre,' said Anton Preisinger, who had played the part of Jesus in 1950 and 1960, 'not theology.' (For good measure he added: 'I played Jesus, which was the greatest honour of my life, and Jesus was a Jew. How should I be anti-Semitic?')

Secondly, it was argued that if the Daisenberger text sometimes made Jesus speak in the dialect of an Oberammergauer, the Rosner text made everyone speak as if they had learned Latin and German poetry in the Ettal school. So, approaching death, Jesus is made to recite to his mother:

> *Leb wohl! Es wird sich alles enden.*
> *Mein Vater will den Engel senden,*
> *Der uns in diesem grossen Werk*
> *Und in dem grossen Leid bestärk.*

> Farewell! Soon all things will end.
> My Father will an angel send
> To help us in this work along,
> And in our sorrow make us strong.

The people of Oberammergau were reluctant to accept such doggerel. In Daisenberger's version, the movingly human Jesus says, as he leaves his mother for the last time: 'For the tender love and motherly care which you have given me in the thirty-three years of my life, receive the thanks of your son. The father calls me. Farewell, best of all mothers.' This is the text which urges the spectator at Christ's burial to 'Stand quietly and watch and see where one can find a love to compare with this.'

Thirdly, the Oberammergauers who supported Daisenberger's text legitimately argued that it was far closer to Holy Scripture than Rosner's text. 'We cannot change what the Bible says,' observed Anton Preisinger.

So for the most part Stephen Schaller's suggestions were rejected. The debate had provoked strong passions on both sides. The Cardinal Archbishop of Munich, Doepfner, while supporting the spirit of the Vatican decree of 1965 insisted that he could only advise the people of Oberammergau and could not dictate to them. Hans Schwaighofer, who had played Judas in the production of 1950 and had been chosen to produce the 1970 Passion Play, resigned when Schaller's proposals were rejected. The American Jewish Congress, a pioneer human relations group founded in 1906, called upon sympathizers to object to what had happened and refuse to support the 1970 production. Among those responding to this call were distinguished Americans such as Arthur Miller, Leonard Bernstein and Lionel Trilling, and from inside Germany writers of the calibre of Günther Grass and Heinrich Böll.

Father Schaller was particularly incensed. 'The Oberammergauers do not wish to be anti-Semitic,' he conceded, adding, 'but the development of history has passed them by.' He also allowed himself the liberty of using the old canard of the profits reaped from the play. 'The locals believe they have one irrefutable argument to prove they are right,' he complained, 'an enormous financial profit at the end of the season, making them the richest village in Bavaria.'

In fact the village itself was extremely concerned about the text of its famous play, and the debate continued. For a time in the 1970s a majority of the village Council supported a return to a modified Rosner text; but this was a decision that the whole village needed to take. After special stage performances of the various options in 1978, a large majority of the villagers voted to keep their nineteenth-century version, but to amend it. Hans Mayr, who was to produce the play in 1980, chaired a committee to vet the Daisenberger text.

The most significant amendment they made was an important and, by now, obvious one. As we have seen, the nineteenth-century text, drawing on a tradition reaching as far back as the medieval miracle plays, made the money-changers driven out of the Temple by Jesus into his chief enemies. These men were depicted stirring up trouble for him among the leading Jews of the time. The device was dramatically effective, no doubt, but it has no basis in the Gospels. And in the context of centuries of anti-Semitism, to point up the role of Jewish money-changers in such an unhistorical fashion could only contribute to the misunderstanding of Jews and Judaism. Hans Mayr and his committee, which included as theological adviser Father Gregor Römmelein of the Ettal monastery, removed the whole offending section.

They also altered the text to emphasize Jesus's own race. Jewish visitors to the Passion Play are now described as 'brothers and sisters from the race from which our Saviour came'. Jesus's followers refer to him as 'Rabbi'.

Thirdly, the committee cut out the unflattering and discourteous references to the Pharisees. What observers like Dean Stanley and Dean Farrar had perceived as fine drama was now seen (in the words of the Protestant Professor Robert G. Davis of Columbia University) as 'naive scoundrelism such as only exists in the movies'.

The Oberammergau Passion Play has become more biblical. Daisenberger fully intended to base his text on the Gospels. But, for instance, he nowhere introduced the concern shown by the Jewish priests at possible reprisals if Jesus and his followers stirred up trouble against the Romans. He underplayed the fact that crucifixion was not a Jewish penalty and that Jesus was in fact put to death by the Romans. In Daisenberger's text, Pontius Pilate shouts at the crowd of Jews, 'The curse of blood be on you and your children', whereas according to St Matthew's Gospel, it is the people who cry, 'His blood be on us and on our children.' The text of 1980 followed the Gospel. And now, instead of the whole crowd calling for the death of Jesus, some of them call for his release.

In a sermon at the opening mass of the 1980 Passion Play season, Cardinal Joseph Ratzinger of Munich insisted that the story of the passion of Jesus is misunderstood if it is seen as anti-Semitic. The sixteenth-century Council of Trent, he observed, said that Christ was crucified as a result of the sinfulness which is displayed by the whole human race, not just one section of it. 'Christ's passion does not ask for revenge,' he preached, 'but for reconciliation.'

Some would have liked the revisers of Daisenberger's text to go further. When the Burgermeister of Oberammergau, Ernst Zwink, invited distinguished representatives of the Anti-Defamation League of B'nai B'rith to visit the village and make their comments personally to him, they said they felt the play could stress still more strongly the Jewishness of Jesus and the complicity of Pontius Pilate in his death.

The Oberammergau community has remained aware of the need constantly to guard against prejudice, however unintentional. In 1983 the villagers paid for their theological adviser, Father Römmelein, to visit the Holy Land in search of greater authenticity for their play. The director of the Anti-Defamation League was invited to suggest further improvements for the text of the 1984 production of the play. That text, for the thirty-seventh Passion Play season, three hundred and fifty years after the village of Oberammergau first re-enacted Christ's passion in accordance with their solemn vow, is officially described as 'revised in 1980 by Father Gregor Römmelein in accordance with Vatican II'.

The Oberammergauers seem able to revise their text as our understanding of God's will develops without losing any of its dramatic power. Patrick O'Donovan, describing the moment in the 1980 play when Jesus, carrying his cross, fell twice, observed, 'the crash of wood on the stage is one of the most terrible sounds I have heard'.

What the 1980 production particularly strove to emphasize was the complicity of all of us in causing such suffering. The Prologue insisted: 'In no way do we wish to look for guilt in others. Let us each recognize his own guilt in these events.' No such words had been heard at Oberammergau before.

Yet it must be said that in the past many spectators at the Oberammergau Passion Play were intelligent enough not to try to place the whole blame for the crucifixion of Jesus on the sins of one section of the human race alone. They too could recognize their own guilt in these events. That passionate Victorian journalist W.T. Stead, after seeing the production of 1890, wrote: 'The Passion Play has at least done this – it sets us discussing the conduct of Caiaphas, Pilate and Judas as if they were our contemporaries, as if they were statesmen at Westminster, judges at the Old Bailey, or administrators in India.' Stead believed that Caiaphas represented 'the great prototype of the domineering and intolerant ecclesiastic all the world over'. He shrewdly added, 'there is a latent Caiaphas in every heart'.

5 Staging the Passion Play

The earliest religious drama of the Christian era took place in the churches themselves. Acts of worship in the fourth century developed rituals and movements which lent passion to the readings of Holy Scripture and to the actions of those who led believers in praise of God.

In the later Middle Ages 'mystery' and 'miracle' plays frequently took place outside churches, although in Oberammergau the play would almost certainly have taken place inside the tiny parish church that was to be rebuilt in the eighteenth century. But long before this rebuilding took place, the fame of the play made the actors move outside the church into the graveyard, where they could perform before the graves of those who had died in the great plague. The church, which seated very few people and held fewer than five hundred standing, proved too small.

Already the villagers felt the need to make some provision for the spectators. In 1674, forty years after their first performance of the Passion Play, a note in the Oberammergau Play Book records that the performance was a great success, and adds, 'in future seats shall be made everywhere for persons who come to see it'.

By the mid eighteenth century, the cemetery was itself too small for the performances. The parish priest, Alois Plutz, directed that the performance of 1750 should take place in a field a little way from his newly built parish church. This field, to the north side of the church, became known as the 'Passion Meadow', and each year a performance was to take place the villagers would erect a stage for their play. Not until 1815 was a more permanent stage built. The designer, the parish priest of the time, was called Nikolaus Umloch. So successful was his design, which included wings and also an apron-stage of the kind still used by the Oberammergau chorus during the Passion Play, that in 1830 Umloch was called back to the village from Garmisch-Partenkirchen (where he then ministered) to help build a larger one in a new 'Passion Meadow' – the site of the present theatre.

The actors, however, still had no dressing-rooms. It was considered enough to rent a nearby room for the actor playing Jesus to change in, while the rest simply used neighbouring cottages. The audience could stand or sit wherever they chose, some of them even perching in trees.

In 1840 an auditorium was finally built. This led indirectly to the practice of having more than one performance in 'Passion years', since the new 'theatre' was far too small for all who wished to see the performance to do so at one sitting. The whole construction, theatre and stage, was now curiously at odds with the biblical play for which it was designed, since it was built in the then fashionable 'Greek' style. But it led the villagers to seek something even more elaborate for their increasingly successful performances.

By 1880 the theatre set had been redesigned. A more triumphant Christ now appears on the pediment and the whole edifice is altogether grander. To the left and right, classical staircases lead to the houses of Pontius Pilate and the High Priest. This photograph of a rehearsal shows the set on the right-hand side as yet unfinished

Conscious now of a responsibility – learned from Father Alois Daisenberger – to the Christian community of Germany and beyond, as well as to their own vow, the villagers sought outside help. In 1890 Karl Lautenschläger of the Munich Court Theatre helped them to design and build what is basically the present theatre. Lautenschläger showed great sensitivity to the old traditions of Oberammergau. He was willing to work closely with Ludwig Lang, who directed the village school of wood-carving. On the left of the stage, seen from the auditorium, broad sweeping steps led up to the house of the High Priest Annas. Matching these on the right were steps leading to the house of Pontius Pilate, Roman procurator at the time of Christ. In the proscenium arch a curtain showed the Old Testament figures, Isaiah, Moses and Jeremiah, and on the pediment above the stage Jesus was depicted blessing children.

Today these scenes have been removed. But the houses of Annas and Pilate remain. Then as now the great apron-stage is open to the elements, giving the spectators an astonishingly beautiful view of the Bavarian Alps, with their sometimes gentle breezes and clouds and their occasional thunderstorms and lightning.

By 1899 Lautenschläger's new theatre was complete. A six-arched hall held 4,200 spectators. For the first time they were completely roofed in.

Thomas Cook's *Excursionist and Tourist Advertiser* for 1900 delightedly announced that the Oberammergau stage had been widened by twenty-five feet under the guidance of the Munich Court Theatre. New scenery and boxes had been provided, at a total cost of some £6,000. Seats, Cook's announced, were reservable at prices of five German marks

In 1890 the fashionable
visitors to Oberammergau
watch a 'living tableau'
depicting the expulsion of
Adam and Eve from the
Garden of Eden

upwards. For the 1930 and 1934 seasons, the theatre was again enlarged. The pediment was adorned with a cross, the Lamb of God and a chalice, flanked by praying angels. This remains the theatre of today.

Its construction – of concrete blocks, with arched girders visible inside, is by no means beautiful. Advertising the Jubilee performances of 1934, Thomas Cook's wrote: 'The theatre itself is roughly like an airport shed.' Little has changed since then. The seats are scarcely upholstered. Yet the theatre has two tremendous virtues. First, every person can see the stage and action perfectly. Secondly, everyone can hear perfectly. This is a small acoustical miracle. The theatre has no disturbing echo or extraneous noises – unlike, say, the far more sophisticated Royal Albert Hall in London, opened in 1871 when, it was noted, the Prince of Wales's speech 'could be heard in all parts of the building; in many parts it could be heard twice'. No actor at the Passion Play needs any artificial amplification for his voice. The actors still play in all weathers; the audience remains dry and, if necessary, the orchestra pit can be covered against rain.

The new theatre of 1930 illustrates not only the growing confidence of Oberammergau after an era of virtual poverty – for the auditorium of 1899 filled the wall-spaces between the great iron arches only with painted canvas, as a measure of economy – but also the extraordinary talents to be found in this small Bavarian village. The new structure followed closely that of Karl Lautenschläger, the Munich professional, but it was constructed almost entirely by local men. The producer of the 1930 play, Georg Lang, drew up the preliminary drawings. Raimund

(*right*) Stage Director Georg
Johann Lang rehearses
Anton Preisinger (Jesus) for
the production of 1950

(*below*) The entry into
Jerusalem on Palm Sunday:
Helmut Fischer plays Christ
in the 1970 production

Lang (the Burgermeister responsible for reviving the play in 1950) produced the final working drawings. Georg Lang sculpted the new design on the pediment, which has now become the symbol of the Passion Play. New dressing-rooms were built. And the main stage was roofed in glass, to provide cover for the 'living tableaux' and the scenes of Christ's passion.

The chorus still stands and sings in fair or foul weather. In bad weather the singers wear underslips made of oilskin, but this does not protect their clothing, and each member has two sets. As an observer of 1934 noted, 'women members of the chorus work under a strain which make their hair in particular suffer severely. The hair comes out in handfuls and never after recovers its former luxuriance.' The same observer concluded: 'It will be seen, therefore, that the villagers are prepared to make real personal sacrifices for the honour of appearing in their Passion Play, and their unselfishness is the measure of their piety.'

The costumes of the chorus are fine, and breathtaking in their variety. The costumes of the leading actors and actresses are remarkable. Until the early nineteenth century these were the only ones kept permanently at Oberammergau. The rest were borrowed, as we know from local account books, from local monasteries and from other villages which performed passion plays.

The design above the proscenium of the modern theatre has become the logo of the Oberammergau Passion Play

Today, however, costumes for the entire cast, amounting to over a thousand garments in all, are kept in the village. Most of them were made by the villagers, sometimes using materials imported from the Orient. Some of the costumes were made to designs found in Palestinian museums. Others use traditional colours evolved over the centuries in Oberammergau. Thus Judas is dressed in yellow (not gold) and black, symbolizing envy and death. A handful of costumes, such as one of the robes of the High Priest, were bought in the Orient, as was the cloak of Joseph of Arimathea which was made in Teheran and cost 800 German marks. Before each Passion Play the women of the village have traditionally worked to repair damaged costumes and to adapt them for the different actors and actresses chosen for the play.

Choosing these players is one of the most jealously guarded Oberammergau rituals. About two years before each 'Passion year', the Burgermeister recites to the village the words of its vow. Then a committee of twenty-four is chosen to elect the players. The Burgermeister by tradition chairs this committee. The parish priest is vice-chairman. The sixteen members of the Council of Oberammergau similarly are members of the election committee as of right. Six others are elected by popular vote.

The first task of the election committee is to attend mass in the parish church. Then they must elect one of their own number to produce the next season's play. That done, on 'election day' they elect 1,200 citizens of Oberammergau to take part.

Only those who have lived in the village for at least twenty years are eligible to play adult parts. In addition, no woman who wishes to take part must be married or aged over thirty-five. Two hundred Oberammergau children are needed for the play. But the chief anxiety of the election committee is to select wisely players for the 123 speaking parts, and especially for the leading roles. Only the producer is allowed to argue about prospective choices. In the event of a tie, he has the casting vote. Formerly voting was with white balls and black balls, to indicate whether an elector approved or disapproved of a candidate. Today the procedure is less formal, though any elector closely related to a candidate is expected to leave while the prospective player is discussed by the others. When the proceedings are finished, the names of the elected players are chalked on a board in the square outside the theatre.

This is always a moment of immense excitement and even rivalry. No one can be certain of being elected. Women who have put off marriage in the hope of securing a part are frequently disappointed. Men who played leading roles in previous productions of the play can never be certain of being elected a second time. The first post-war election in 1949 was one of exceptional tension. Disagreement over who should play the role of Jesus actually delayed the election – an almost unprecedented occurrence. In the end the part went to Anton Preisinger, thus 'deposing' the Lang family whose sons had played Jesus since 1900. Anton Preisinger's sister had played the role of Mary Magdalene in 1930; in 1950 that role was taken by the twenty-four-year-old Gabriele Gropper. The other leading woman's role, that of the Virgin Mary, was taken by Annemarie Mayr, one of whose family had played the part of Jesus in 1870-71, 1880 and 1890.

1. Rudolph Zwinck, playing Jesus in 1980, rides into Jerusalem on the first Palm Sunday.

4. *(above)* Rudolph Zwinck as Christ raises the bread in blessing at the Last Supper.
St John sits beside him and St Peter looks on.

2. *(top left)* Jesus overthrows the tables of the money-changers in the Temple (1980.)

3. *(bottom left)* Jesus and his disciples at the Last Supper in the 1980 production.

7. (*above*) Rudolph Zwinck as Christ carrying the Cross to Golgotha.

5. (*top left*) Judas betrays Jesus with a kiss. The 1980 production displays the traditional Oberammergau skill in deploying many actors on the stage of the Passion Play theatre.

6. (*bottom left*) A 'living tableau' from the 1980 production: Joseph is presented to the Egyptians as a saviour.

8. Jesus, crowned with thorns and bearing a reed as a sceptre, is mocked as a king. (Rudolph Zwinck in 1980.)

9. Jesus crucified between two thieves: Oberammergau, 1980.

11. Mary holds the body of her dead son.

10. (*opposite*) The Virgin Mary (Martha Wiedemann) and Mary Magdalene (Theresia Feliner)
at the foot of the Cross: Oberammergau, 1980.

13. Traditional frescoes on a house in Oberammergau.

12. *(opposite)* The risen Christ appears before Mary Magdalene in the production of 1980.

15. Schloss Linderhof, built for Ludwig and completed in 1879.
Here the King entertained and rewarded the leading
Oberammergau actors of 1871.

14. *(opposite)* Portrait of King Ludwig II of Bavaria by G. Schachinger.
Ludwig was chief patron of the Passion Play
in the seasons of 1870–71 and 1880.

17. Schloss Hohenschwangau, built by Ludwig II's father on a medieval foundation,
where the future patron of the Passion Play spent much of his unhappy childhood.

16. *(opposite)* Schloss Neuschwanstein: the fairy-tale castle built opposite Schloss Hohenschwangau
by Ludwig II and never completed.

18. The peacock throne at Linderhof. Ludwig II preferred the peacock, a symbol of peace, to the flag, a symbol of war.

(*above*) The crucifixion as depicted in 1890

(*top left*) Hugo Rutz as St Peter in 1950

(*below left*) Alois Lang, who played Jesus in 1934, singing the 'prologue' in 1950

Although the villagers of Oberammergau eschew the notions of 'stardom' and 'personality', those who play the role of Jesus – and especially those who play the part for more than one season – inevitably become famous. When Eduard Devrient saw Tobias Flunger play Jesus in 1850, he declared this to be one of 'the purest and most peaceful experiences' of his life. Flunger, in a violet robe with a red cloak thrown over it, rode out of the crowd on an ass. 'The line of his pale face, his fine straight nose, his noble forehead, his parted hair and his beard,' wrote Devrient, 'were in every detail consonant with the pictures of Christ which artists have impressed on our minds through the ages.'

The Jesus of Oberammergau as the role has developed since Devrient's day is a less sentimental but no less impressive figure. Each actor who plays the role has added his own insights to the tradition. Anton Lang, playing the role for three seasons at the beginning of the twentieth century, stressed the gentleness of Christ. His successor Alois Lang, in contrast, tried to emphasize the heroism of Jesus. Anton Preisinger's return to the style of Anton Lang in the 1950 season must have seemed more fitting to many of the Oberammergauers, for he was re-elected to play the part of Jesus in the 1960 season.

Much depends on the looks (and therefore also the age) of would-be actors, for at Oberammergau the only make-up used in the Passion Play is that simulating the blood of Jesus. For the rest, the actors (save for the clean-shaven Pontius Pilate) must grow their beards and hair to the length demanded by the parts they are to play. As a result, Oberammergau in the year before a Passion Play season is filled with men who look slightly unkempt. This refusal to allow make-up is frequently the reason for a man or a woman's failure to attain a desired role in an

The theatre as it is today: the 'prologue' and choir rehearse their roles

Oberammergau season. It is said that Joseph Mayr, who managed to control his hot-blooded character enough to play a remarkable Jesus in the last three seasons of the nineteenth century, was bitterly disappointed when prematurely greying hair lost him the role in 1900. On the other hand, actors who have played leading roles in the past are usually extremely happy to take lesser roles later on. Alois Lang, who played Jesus in 1930 and 1934, sang a fine Prologue in 1950 and was content to play the minor role of Simon of Bethany in 1960.

One very recent change has helped to do away with the understandable but slightly unseemly rivalry in the quest for parts – though the change came about for other reasons. Until the 1980 season, leading players were assigned understudies to replace them in time of sickness or accident. One unhappy replacement was that of Peter Rendel, who was to play St Peter but died in March 1934. His replacement, Hubert Mayr (who had been elected to play the role of St James), was the youngest St Peter in Oberammergau's recorded history. In 1980, after much heart-searching, the Passion Play committee decided to elect two actors to play each leading role at alternate performances. The innovation looked like causing production difficulties. Instead it worked splendidly, each actor naturally giving a slightly different emphasis to his role from that of his partner.

To ease the tension before election day, Oberammergauers have frequently joked that the only 'stars' who never jostle for attention are the animals who yearly take part in the production. The sheep involved are the pet lambs of the village; the village donkey can always secure a part as the ass which carried Christ into Jerusalem. As for the doves used by the money-changers in the Temple, these are local homing-pigeons.

This photograph of the 'living tableau' of the expulsion from Eden (complete with the serpent coiled round the tree) shows the accuracy of the engraver's representation on page 45

Jesus overturns the long-used cage when he appears in the Temple, the pigeons escape, fly out through the open-air apron-stage, return home and are brought back by their owners for the next performance.

The orchestra of sixty players and the chorus of sixteen male and thirty female voices were traditionally trained in Oberammergau by the village schoolmaster – Rochus Dedler's successor. Even now the children of the village are encouraged to sing and play musical instruments at a very early age, both at school and in the evenings. The connection between school and Passion Play remains close in Oberammergau. Hans Schwaighofer, for instance, who played in the orchestra of 1934 when he was only fourteen years old, later became a village schoolmaster. But the tradition of the schoolmaster training the musicians was broken in 1950, when Schwaighofer took the role of Judas in the play. With the welcome help of Eugen Pabst, a sculptor named Ulrich Hohenleitner (who had played first violin in the orchestra) took charge of the music.

If passions have run high at times within Oberammergau, the play has also provoked jealousy outside. Detractors of the plays have described Oberammergau as the richest village in Bavaria. Dean Farrar recorded a critic who said in 1890 that there was no religion at all about the Passion Play; it was purely 'a monetary speculation'.

Oberammergau has never mounted its Passion Play for nothing, as it were. From the start the performances were a thank-offering to God, but as such they were costly enough. The account-books which survive record that in 1701 the villagers paid twelve florins and thirty Kreutzers to Bernhard Steinle for rehearsing and directing the Passion Play. In the same year, nineteen florins were paid to Sebastian Würmser and Martin Faistenmantel, painters, for their wages and materials. The village had to pay for its gunpowder, which simulated thunder. In 1701 this cost twelve Kreutzers. And the hire of trumpeters from Ettal to play at the 1700 performance cost two florins.

Such payments continued with each successive fulfilment of the vow of 1633. For a long time the village borrowed from neighbouring Unterammergau the donkey on which Jesus rode into Jerusalem. In 1820, 'for all the performances together', the hire of this donkey cost nine florins and thirteen Kreutzers. In the same year appears an entry in the account-book: 'To Sarah Bierting for preparing the meals for the scene with Simon of Bethany, fourteen florins and forty-two Kreutzers.' The producers also believed that Jesus's Last Supper with his disciples ought to be a proper meal. Entries in the account-books reveal that they had to pay the local butcher and other merchants for the food consumed during this scene.

The Last Supper as performed in 1890 shows the influence of Leonardo da Vinci

Oberammergau began to ask richer visitors to pay for the best seats at the Passion Play only in 1790. Not until 1860 were the actors properly paid in order to make up for their loss of earnings because they were obliged to abandon their usual occupations during the season of the play. In that year the bill amounted to 760 florins in all. Until then the actors were simply given a special treat. The account-book of 1701 records ten florins paid to the actors, 'so that they might have a drink following the traditional custom'.

But as the Passion Play flourished (and audiences in 1960 totalled over one million people), some accused the village and its inhabitants of simple greed. An anonymous pamphlet of 1891 bore the title, 'The Opulence of Oberammergau'.

Of course some people have tried to cash in on the Passion Play.

Thomas Cook's advance publicity for the 1900 season warned against these. 'Rooms in private houses in the best and healthiest part of the village have been placed at our disposal,' announced Cook's *Excursionist and Tourist Advertiser*, 'where the visitors can partake of all their meals comfortably, without being under the necessity of scrambling for them at third-rate inns (so-called hotels) or temporary refreshment booths, which are unavoidably overcrowded.' In the last quarter of the twentieth century on my visits to Oberammergau I have never personally found any third-rate inns in which to 'scramble' for my food, and there are no parts of the village that even the most fastidious visitor could describe as unhealthy. If there was ever any truth in the allegations of Thomas Cook's brochure of 1900, this was no longer the case by 1930. After visiting Oberammergau in that year, Mme Suzanne St Barbe Baker reported: 'At the time of the play the village is crowded, although there are quite a number of hotels and smaller inns. But the householders let all their spare rooms, and I can assure you that they are just as good hosts as they are actors. Your room will be clean, and you can count on a very good breakfast, even on the days when the performances take place.' And today, even with so many visitors passing through the village during Passion Play seasons, Oberammergau remains extraordinarily welcoming, cheerful and clean.

Thomas Cook's took up the defence of Oberammergau before the season of 1934. 'The people of Oberammergau have never been a grasping people,' said Cook's *American Traveller's Gazette*, 'and they are particularly anxious that no one shall be kept away on the score of expense. In this they are supported by the German Government and the authorities of the State Railways have made substantial reductions in the fares.' Cook's, charging in that year £8. 19s. 6d. for the return journey to Oberammergau, without an overnight stay and without a ticket for the play, were legitimately aiming to make a profit themselves and are perhaps not the best witnesses for the defence of Oberammergau. But in fact the villagers have never been paid more than would serve to make up what they lose from neglecting their ordinary work by appearing in the play. They have been careful to reserve certain rights for themselves, such as that of photographing performances. (When the British crusading journalist W. T. Stead took his Kodak into a performance in 1890, he reported that he was spotted taking photographs by Caiaphas from the stage, who alerted attendants to confiscate his plates!) But they have resolutely refused all offers to make themselves rich by taking their play outside their Bavarian village.

Hollywood tried and failed to persuade them to make a film of the Passion Play. After the triumphant performances of 1871, the actors refused the huge sum of sixty thousand florins to take the play to Vienna. Their vow was that they would for ever enact the passion, death and resurrection of Jesus in Oberammergau, not anywhere else. Joseph Mayr, who could have played the role of Jesus in Vienna (and had been paid only £13 for his superlative performances in 1871), contemptuously rejected the invitation with the words, 'If they want to remove our play from Oberammergau, they must take with it the peak of the Kofel and its guardian cross.'

6 The World comes to Oberammergau

In the three and a half centuries since the Oberammergauers were spared the plague by the mercy of God, they have suffered their fair share of human calamities. The valley of the Ammer has suffered from the wars that have at times devastated Europe. The criticisms which led to attempts to ban their Passion Play were not the only charges of duplicity, greed or foolishness levelled at the villagers. Over the centuries faithfulness to their vow has enabled them to overcome sometimes enormous difficulties.

The village has not always prospered. In 1740, for instance, the harvest failed in the Ammer valley. Crops were ruined again the following year, when the river flooded, and in that year too half the village was burned to the ground. The Oberammergauers escaped the social unrest which, partly as a result of European famine, led to the Revolution of 1789 in France, and the eventual rise to power of Napoleon Bonaparte. But they could not entirely escape the consequences of Napoleon's ambition. In 1800 the village of Oberammergau was bombarded and looted by French troops. In that year only five performances of the play were given to fulfil the vow.

The brilliance of Othmar Weiss's text and Rochus Dedler's music set the Passion Play on the way to greater success. In 1840 eight or nine thousand spectators saw the Passion Play, performed in July by three hundred and fifty of the villagers. The play that year lasted from eight o'clock in the morning till four o'clock in the afternoon.

Clearly the play was changing its character. In emending Othmar Weiss's text, the local parish priest Alois Daisenberger realized that he was addressing a wider audience than the villagers and their counterparts from the neighbouring Bavarian villages. The Passion Play was becoming famous. Some acute observers feared that this would ruin it. Dean Stanley, the biographer of Thomas Arnold of Rugby, went to see the performance of 1860. He was entranced. But he commented, 'The best wish that can be offered for the continuance of the play is that it may remain alone of its kind, and that it may never attract any large additional influx of spectators from distant regions or uncongenial circles.'

When Stanley made that judgement, Oberammergau was still a remote village, difficult for visitors to reach. As its fame increased, hundreds of carriages blocked the road to the village during the play season. They edged their way up the steep mountain path, nose to tail, and on dangerous descents they sometimes ran into each other.

But none of this now deterred would-be spectators – particularly the intrepid British – who flocked to Oberammergau in increasing numbers. In 1870 a celebrated British clergyman, Canon Malcolm MacColl, visited

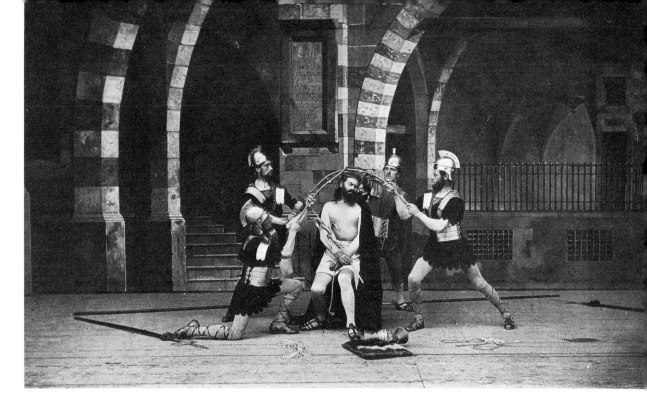

Joseph Mayr, playing Jesus in 1890, is crowned with thorns

Oberammergau. His account of the Passion Play ran into three editions before a year was out. MacColl detailed the expenses of the journey for his fellow-countrymen who might like to see the performances for themselves. The costs were:

London to Cologne: second class	£2. 9s. 0d.
Extra: first class on steamer	5s. 0d.
First class difference, Vivriers to Cologne	5s. 10d.
Cologne to Bingen by steamer (first class)	6s. 0d.
Bingen to Nuremberg: second class	16s. 0d.
Nuremberg to Munich: second class	11s. 0d.
Munich to Weilheim: second class	2s. 6d.
Weilheim to Oberammergau by carriage and pair	£1. 1s. 0d.

The whole journey, Canon MacColl calculated, cost a mere £5. 16s. 4d. The railway age was opening up Oberammergau to the world. 'Hotel expenses are, of course, a matter of taste,' he observed, 'but if wines are dispensed with, six shillings a day will easily cover everything.'

Scarcely had the season of 1870 begun when it was again interrupted by war. After sixteen performances, members of the cast were called up for military service in the Franco-Prussian War. Even Joseph Mayr, who was playing Jesus, was called up. Fortunately, King Ludwig of Bavaria intervened to make sure that Mayr never reached the front. The Oberammergau actor was given barrack duties in Munich, and was never sent to France. He managed not to shave off the beard and cut the long hair he had grown for his central part in the Passion Play. He was spared the fate of some of his fellow-villagers, who were killed on the battlefield.

On 28 January 1871 the French were defeated. The villagers decided to continue the season of 1870 one year late. In one sense the delay worked in their favour. Canon MacColl's book on the performance he had seen, as well as his articles about the village in *The Times*, had given great publicity to Oberammergau among the English middle and upper classes. Even the British royal family was fascinated by the events in the little Bavarian village. The future king Edward VII travelled there with his bride, and they stayed in the house of Joseph Mayr himself. (At their coronation Mayr, who was a wood-carver, sent the royal pair a model of Leonardo da Vinci's 'Last Supper'. Edward sent the former Christ of Oberammergau a silver medal.) Edward and Alexandra travelled to Oberammergau supposedly incognito, as Baron and Baroness Renfrew. Although he spoke German fluently (in fact he spoke English with a pronounced German accent), the future king was too well-known a figure for this ruse to succeed. His visit greatly publicized the Passion Play. Altogether nineteen extra performances were staged in 1871.

Now the enterprising young travel firm of Thomas Cook's was promoting the play. Exactly thirty years earlier Thomas Cook, a printer in Leicester, had hired a train to take five hundred enthusiasts to a temperance rally at Loughborough. He made a profit on the venture, and within a few years was organizing trips to Scotland, Ireland and Wales.

Thomas Cook's had their first taste of the Continent in 1855 when the firm organized a visit to the great Paris Exhibition of that year, combining it with a tour of Germany. Their tours took in Switzerland and Italy by the 1860s, and in that decade the company realized the potential of religious pilgrimages. In 1869 a tour organized by Thomas Cook reached Jerusalem and the Holy Land. In 1871 the company ran its first visit to the Oberammergau Passion Play.

For the 1880 season the number of people wishing to visit Oberammergau was so large that Thomas Cook sent a special representative to stay in the village and look after his clients. By that year a railway had been opened between Munich and Murnau, a village less than fifteen miles from Oberammergau, and by 1890 this railway had reached Garmisch-Partenkirchen.

The Bavarians also decided that something must be done to improve the dangerous road from Garmisch to Oberammergau. An English lady, Mary Trench, after visiting the 1890 play, reported that a 'magnificent new road, one long zig-zag', had been made in 1889. This road was in fact macadamized and eighteen feet wide. Small wonder that Thomas Cook's were asked to transport about six thousand visitors to the Passion Play in that year. The firm set up its office in the present garden of Becker's Laundry – Faistmantlgasse no. 2 – to arrange tickets and lodgings for this throng of British visitors.

Thomas Cook's angrily refuted suggestions made in *The Times* and elsewhere that they were profiteering from religion. At the same time the firm shrewdly became an 'official representative' of the village on behalf of its Passion Play. By 1900 an electric railway could bring spectators from Munich to Oberammergau very early in the morning and take them back the same day after they had seen the play. But Thomas Cook's

The deposition: Jesus played by Anton Lang in 1900

Mary mourns Jesus: a *pietà* of 1890

pointed out that the railway charged a higher price for this service; they recommended visitors to stay in Oberammergau itself, and offered to find them accommodation. The publicity put out by the travel firm in 1900 added: 'We can also dispose of apartments with sitting-rooms, which have been retained in former years by various royal personages, at prices to be arranged.'

After their stay in Oberammergau, tourists could now travel to Murnau by electric tramcars to continue their sightseeing.

The Passion Play, still following the pattern set by Weiss and Daisenberger and still performed by the villagers and no one else, was nevertheless now big business. In 1910 thirty-one performances were scheduled, but in the end the actors were required to perform fifty-six times. Around five thousand spectators watched each performance. Thomas Cook's placed interpreters in uniform on the trains running between London and the Bavarian village, and charged between eleven and thirty-six guineas for their tours (or 'pilgrimages', as they called them). Twenty years before, visitors had been obliged to secure lodgings with the villagers and then queue for tickets on the day of the performance, with no certainty of finding a good seat. Now the visitor's every need could be catered for in advance.

Within four years Britain and Germany were at war. The First World War bankrupted the Germans and destroyed the governments of defeated nations. Oberammergau shared in the tragedy. Between 1914 and 1918 sixty-seven of its sons were killed in battle and many more were wounded. Once well-off, the envy of some of their neighbours, the villagers now shared in the poverty caused by inflation and the huge reparations demanded by the victorious allies.

Yet the Oberammergauers were determined once again to keep their vow. Between May and September of 1922 forty principal performances of the Passion Play took place, and these were not enough to cater for the demand. A further twenty-eight extra performances were required to accommodate altogether 310,000 spectators.

Germany was not yet financially secure. Indeed, the black year of 1929 plunged her into a greater depression. Yet in the following year the villagers performed their play eighty times. Over 70,000 more spectators came than in the season of 1922.

In 1933 Adolf Hitler came to power in Germany. To many, Christians as well as non-Christians, he seemed to bring new life to a dispirited Germany. The full horrors of his regime were yet to be revealed. The aged hero Hindenburg, himself a devout Christian, had given Hitler his blessing, and many, including the villagers of Oberammergau, felt that the nation was poised for spiritual renewal. The year 1934 was the tercentenary of the very first fulfilment of their vow. They decided to produce a Passion Play in 1934 as great and devout as any before.

It was a tremendous success. Daisenberger's text was now set in three acts with twenty 'living tableaux'; it lasted from eight in the morning till six in the evening, with a two-hour interval. The special Jubilee commemoration volume issued by the villagers promised that 'should the throng on any of the days of performance be such that the accommodation of the theatre be too small, the play will be given on the following day in the same way'. In all, eighty-four performances were needed, to cope with over 400,000 visitors.

Today it is ironic to look back at the high hopes placed by the villagers of Oberammergau in their new Führer. They quoted what now seemed prescient words of Eduard Devrient: 'When once the day of promise dawns, when all the German tribes feel again that they are one people, when all our forces will be free, then the old spirit of the people and its art will be filled with new life such as will create wonderful feasts: then the Passion Play of Oberammergau will be remembered again.'

Not content with producing eighty-four performances, the villagers commissioned a famous writer named Leo Weismantel to create for them a drama based on the story of their vow. Weismantel's play, set to music, was judged by most visitors to be a splendid bonus at the 1934 season – even though he took enormous liberties with the true history of the vow. His aim was to portray the birth of Oberammergau as 'a pilgrimage shrine'. In his version of the events of 1633, everyone is dying of the plague *except* Kaspar Schisler. Seeing the village approaching certain doom, Schisler orders his son to carry a great crucifix to the cemetery. Then, to everyone's amazement, the wooden Christ speaks there and then the seven sentences from the cross recorded in the four Gospels. The whole village is healed, and the villagers make their historic vow. 'The play closes,' remarked Thomas Cook's *American Traveller's Gazette* for 1934, 'with music that seems to come out of eternity.'

The joy of 1934 was not to last. Before the performance of 1940 could be cast, Hitler had brought a munitions factory to Oberammergau; before it could be performed, he had led his country into a second disastrous World War. In 1944 the S.S. occupied Schloss Linderhof. The following year the Americans took Oberammergau – fortunately without a struggle. The village and its environs had survived.

The Americans wanted to see another Passion Play. So did the Burgermeister of Oberammergau, Raimund Lang. The difficulties were once more immense. Apart from German poverty after the war, 2,200 refugees from East Germany and the Sudetenland were billeted in barracks in the village and needed caring for – enormously straining the local resources. But the Oberammergauers intended to fulfil their historic vow once again. The occupying Americans helped with building materials for the new production. In 1950 the thirty-fourth season of the Oberammergau Passion Play went ahead and a record number of over half a million visitors came to see it.

Gradually Oberammergau recovered from the wounds caused by Hitler and the Second World War. The 1950 season had revealed that, in spite of what had happened between 1939 and 1945, the play was still a source of healing between the nations, and Oberammergau itself still a place of pilgrimage. Of the 520,000 visitors who saw the play ten years later, over half came from abroad – and of these, forty per cent were British and twenty-five per cent American.

Today the Passion Play is once again securely established. In faithfulness to their vow the villagers have overcome the stresses of three and a half sometimes turbulent centuries.

The Passion Play in a sense now belongs to the world. But it still remains essentially the Passion Play of that Bavarian village. The distinguished English dean, F. W. Farrar, shrewdly observed in 1890 after his visit to the Passion Play: 'When it degenerates into a European spectacle, criticized in all the newspapers by hundreds of reporters as though it were an opera in Dresden or Vienna, it becomes, alas, a fatal anachronism.' Farrar's anxieties were not unreasonable. At the dress rehearsal of the 1890 play, he had seen nearly 600 reporters from most of the countries of the western world.

Farrar found the simplicity of the village and its inhabitants an essential part of the whole Oberammergau achievement. In 1890 he stayed at the house of Joseph Mayr, following the example of the Prince and Princess of Wales in 1871. Mayr, who was still only forty-two years old, was playing the part of Jesus for the third time. Dean Farrar found his home in Oberammergau 'humble but exquisitely clean'. Returning to Mayr's house during the interval, he was delighted to find one of the members of the angel chorus waiting on him at lunch!

At the same time, this cultivated Englishman was immensely impressed by the performance of the play. At four o'clock on the morning of the dress rehearsal a cannon was fired, after street bands had played for most of the previous evening. An hour later the parish church of Oberammergau was crowded for a full choral high mass sung for all who were to take part in the play. Less than two hours later Farrar was among

Portraying mystery: a 'living tableau' of the resurrection

5,000 spectators, waiting for the performance to begin. At eight o'clock a cannon was again fired, and immediately the chorus formed a large semi-circle in front of the stage, all crowned, dressed in green, violet, blue, orange, brown, red and crimson, with the Prologue in glowing scarlet.

Farrar was entranced. He noted the faithfulness of the play to the Bible. Whereas, for instance, at the high mass those few who had received Holy Communion partook only of the bread and not the wine, Farrar observed that the Last Supper as portrayed on the Oberammergau stage showed Jesus giving bread to each of his disciples and the disciples themselves passing round to each other the cup of wine. There was here no alteration to fit in with later Catholic practices. Indeed, Farrar had only one criticism of the play; he did not believe in 'turning men's thoughts habitually to a Christ dying or dead, rather than to Him who is alive for evermore'. The final living tableau of the Passion Play, showing Jesus's ascension to heaven, did not convince this English Christian.

This is a criticism some still make. Perhaps there are some events, such as the resurrection, which are impossible to portray in earthly terms. On the other hand, the play is not something static or fossilized: it is a living tradition, constantly re-created. It may be that in productions to come the villagers will succeed in the almost impossible task of depicting this, the greatest Christian mystery.

What is certain is that today the visitor to the Passion Play sees what Dean Farrar and countless others have seen: a group of men and women, none of them a 'star', all of them sharing a Bavarian humility, uniting in fulfilment of their forefathers' vow to produce a living masterpiece of religious drama that is for many people also an act of worship.

7 A Bavarian Village

Oberammergau's magnificent setting was created by melting ice. When the last great Ice Age retreated, around 120,000 years ago, it left behind the valley of the river Ammer at the foot of the Bavarian Alps. Here today the village of Oberammergau lies, 2,750 feet above sea-level. On the south side of the village, the peak of Mount Kofel, surmounted by a huge cross, reaches 4,400 feet. To the west is the Sonnerberg range, with the peak known as the Pürschling reaching 4,650 feet. To the east towers the Laber, 4,700 feet high. And on a clear day one can see as far as the Zugspitze, Germany's highest peak.

As the Roman empire spread northwards, the legions used Oberammergau as a staging post, naming it Ad Coveliacus, from which today's name Kofel is derived. The Romans brought Christianity to the valley, though perhaps not of a deeply committed kind, for we know that around the middle of the eighth century a missionary called Thasso was busy converting the inhabitants of the region.

Situated on an important route from Italy north through the Alps, the village prospered. The Ammergauers claimed the right to guide all travellers through the valley. In the Middle Ages they would celebrate betrothals and weddings on the Kofel peak itself. Merchants from Nuremberg presented a huge statue of a knight to be erected on the peak, but soon this was replaced by a colossal cross. This cross, made of wood, was itself frequently replaced. When lightning struck it in 1807, it blazed for ten days.

The Reformation scarcely touched this part of Catholic Europe, and today many of the religious customs of the Middle Ages survive in Oberammergau, as in the other villages of the valley. On the morning of the feast of Corpus Christi, for instance, the bells of the parish church ring out for half an hour to announce a solemn procession, in which the parish priest bears a consecrated host, under a canopy, to an altar erected today outside the Passion theatre. The parish musicians lead the procession. Many citizens dress in traditional costume (the livery of the Prince Bishops of Freising, in whose domain Oberammergau lay until 1803). The men wear leather kneebreeches, grey jackets, embroidered braces over white shirts, and coloured silk neckerchiefs. Girls wear full blue skirts, with white blouses and lace-edged petticoats, as well as white hand-knitted stockings and black silver-buckled shoes. The parish priest reads the biblical accounts of the feeding of the five thousand by Jesus and the first Christian eucharist. A choir sings responses and hymns.

At other times of the year the villagers enjoy more secular traditions. The Thursday before the third Sunday in Advent is called *Klopfersnacht* in these parts (i.e. 'the night for knocking on doors'). As evening falls,

A 'living tableau' of the ascension

children go about the village singing songs of Mary and Joseph – who found no room at the inn in Bethlehem – knocking on people's doors as the parents of Jesus may have done. The secular aspect of this ceremony arises when anyone opens a door to the children, who immediately ask for a tip, using the old dialect words, '*I bitt Enk um an Oklopfat*'. A similar mixture of sacred and secular occurs on New Year's Eve, when old and young (in separate processions) wander through the village singing for and blessing the inhabitants, who in turn are expected to hand over money.

The Oberammergauers have not lost their power to create such festivities. One of the most recent in origin occurs on 24 August each year. This, the eve of the feast of St Louis, was also the eve of the birthday (in 1845) of mad King Ludwig II of Bavaria, who was a great patron and benefactor of Oberammergau. On the morning of the 24th young men from the village climb the Kofel and its adjacent mountain slopes, carrying logs and firewood. As night falls these are lighted, to create a blazing crown, a blazing cross and the legend 'L II'. Then the citizens, bearing torches, process behind the brass band to the town centre for a display of fireworks and rockets.

Although there are countless signs here and in the whole region advertising lodgings ('Gaststätte', 'Gasthaus', 'Pension', 'Zimmer', 'Zimmer frei', 'Fremdenzimmer', 'Gasthof', 'Ammergauerhof', 'Hotel', 'Zimmer mit Bad', 'Zimmer mit Dusch', and so on) tourism has not spoiled Oberammergau. Many guesthouses and hotels still retain the old, beautifully tiled stoves (*Kachelöfen*), even though every place is now centrally heated. In every hotel and guesthouse is still to be seen the traditional host's table, the *Stammtisch*, often a very intricately carved table, and invariably without a table-cloth. Sometimes a finely wrought

Before and after: (*top*) boys in Oberammergau letting their hair grow long in preparation for the Passion Play; (*below*) at the end of the Passion Play season, actors queue to have their hair cut. (Note the actor with shorn locks standing on the right)

metal ornament announces that this is the *Stammtisch*. Here the landlord sits with his cronies and chosen friends at the end of an evening. At the other tables his guests are served traditional Bavarian food, *Schnitzel*, for example, and often *Spätzle* (small egg noodles, soft and very gently cooked). Oberammergau may be Bavaria's richest village, but it remains essentially a humble, unspoilt Bavarian village for all that. Its wealth has been used to improve its amenities. A cable-car lifts visitors to the peak of the Laber, with its breathtaking views, and ski-lifts cater for winter sports.

The villagers also used the profits of the Passion Play to create an extraordinary swimming pool – the Wellenbad. After the 1934 Jubilee performances, an alpine pool over 4,500 square metres in dimension was built to replace the simple pool of 1908. Forty years later the profits of the 1970 performances had transformed this into an extraordinary swimming complex, with a heated indoor pool and sauna as well as a heated outdoor pool and a remarkable circular pool with simulated waves. Today it is possible to bathe happily in bikini or swimsuit in the open air, surrounded by snow-clad mountain slopes.

After the turmoils of the Napoleonic wars, Oberammergau began to prosper again in the mid nineteenth century. Wood-carving, which was flourishing in the nearby monastery of Rottenbuch as early as the twelfth century, soon spread to Oberammergau, which had its own guild of master-carvers by the sixteenth century. Their fame extended throughout Germany. Today in the middle of the village can be seen a carving of an eighteenth-century pedlar, carrying on his back a huge wooden tray with plaques, crucifixes, statues and other carvings. Such men carried the work of the Oberammergau wood-carvers throughout Germany and

Wood-carving: the second industry of Oberammergau

(*right*) A member of the Oberammergau school of wood-carving

(*below*) Hans Schwaighofer (Judas in 1950) examines a wood-carving of the nativity

even as far as Russia and the east. The family of Josef Lang, who settled in Oberammergau in 1736, brought a unique business acumen to the trade. The Lang family took care to train young men in the profession, and in 1886 set up a state school to promote their craft. Josef Lang's last direct descendant founded an Art and Culture Museum which on his death in 1921 was acquired by the whole village. Here today the visitor can see the finest examples of this Bavarian art.

Oberammergau wood-carvers today work mostly in spruce, though they also use alder, beech, sycamore and lime. In past years their products were painted or coloured by other means, but today their work, though intricately carved, is otherwise austerely plain. And in the mid eighteenth century another famous tradition began. The Oberammergauers started to carve Christmas cribs. Until then these had been made of paper and cloth (some of these can still be seen in the Oberammergau museum). In 1760, however, the wood-carvers made the first crib for their parish church. For the next eighty years they remodelled and re-created this crib. They dressed the figures in silks and jewellery, copying the details from the costumes of the Passion Play itself. Today this crib is one of the

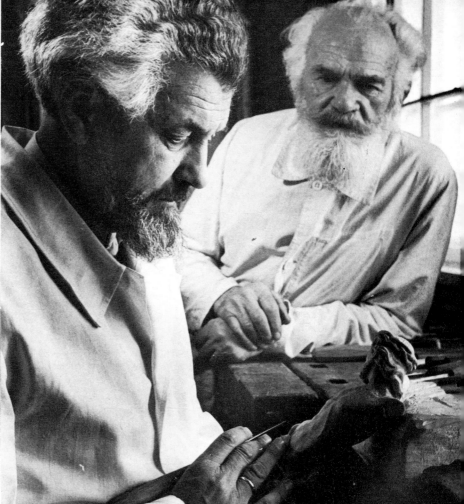

(*right*) Players of 1950 work
on a crucified Christ

(*below*) Willy Bierling
(St John in 1934) carves
a Madonna and Child

most precious exhibits of the museum; it is of priceless historical interest.
But alongside it are innumerable children's toys, dolls, jig-saws, soldiers,
battle scenes, crosses, dolls' houses and furniture, as well as model
fortresses and real clock-cases. Innumerable shops sell modern versions
of the crib, carved with the same skill.

Two aspects of this wood-carving are especially striking. First, in spite
of its skill, it is essentially homely. This could be said to be true of
virtually the whole village. Oberammergau has never lost its roots in the
German countryside. In the very middle of the village the wholesome
smell of cattle leads the visitor to a cowshed, still in use. Opposite the
byre are some of the famous painted houses of the area. The old Bavarian
term for this kind of fresco painting is 'air painting' (*Lüftlmalerei*). The
term derives from the home of the greatest of all these wall-painters,
Franz Zwinck, who lived at Oberammergau in what was known as the
'Airy House', the *Lüftlhaus*. Franz Zwinck was born in 1748 and learned
the technique of fresco painting from church decorators. By the mid
eighteenth century, drawing on the skills of Italians as well as on their
own native traditions, these artists were transforming the interiors of

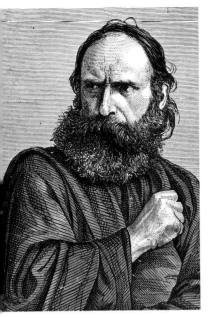

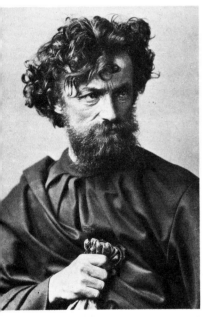

The betrayer:
(*top*) Georg Lechner as
Judas (1880); and (*below*) the
thirty pieces of silver (1890)

churches and monasteries throughout this part of Bavaria in a most remarkable way. They delighted in tricking the eyes of the spectator, creating perspectives so cunning that the painted pillars and vistas seemed three-dimensional. The domes of the churches they decorated seem to open up to the skies and into heaven.

Franz Zwinck applied their techniques to decorating the humble as well as the larger homes of the Oberammergauers. He worked with remarkable speed. Once, it is said, he promised to paint a portrait of the Virgin Mary on the wall of a peasant's house before she could churn a pail of butter. If he succeeded, he should have the butter. If he failed, then she would have her wall-painting for nothing. Of course Franz Zwinck won.

Today his pictures have faded a little. But the visitor can still easily make out the 'Pilate's House', which he started painting in 1769. Here on the garden side is Jesus before the Roman procurator; and the same house boasts an elaborate spiral staircase, apparently three-dimensional, which is a fresco by Zwinck. But Zwinck did not confine himself to religious subjects; other houses were decorated with hunting scenes. The charm he displayed was handed on to his successors. Among the latest wall-paintings in the village are scenes from Hansel and Gretel and Little Red Riding Hood, which decorate the local orphanages.

Zwinck was only forty-three when he died in 1792. A note in the local register of burials observed: 'A painter worthy of the highest praise has ceased to paint.' The parish priest of the time added that in his last illness Zwinck was fortified by the sacraments of the Church. The religious aspect of his life and work was also shared by the wood-carvers of Oberammergau, for along with the essential homeliness of the wood-carvings and paintings of Oberammergau goes a deep spirituality. For the village, in spite of its gaiety and charm, is dominated inevitably by the passion, death and resurrection of Jesus. The village of Oberammergau was built, not around its famous Passion Play theatre (erected only in the present century), but around its parish church; and this church is one of the architectural masterpieces of the whole region.

Oberammergau possessed its own parish church certainly from the twelfth century. Five hundred years later this church was in such disrepair that most of it had to be pulled down.

It was a fortunate moment to begin rebuilding. Living nearby, and at the pinnacle of his career, was one of the greatest of Bavarian rococo architects, Joseph Schmuzer. Schmuzer had already won renown for his magnificent churches at Donauwörth, Garmisch and Augsburg. In 1736 he was commissioned to build a new church, dedicated to St Peter and St Paul, in Oberammergau.

He brought to the task all the arts of Bavarian rococo. Inside the new church, delicate plasterwork merges with multicoloured frescoes, graceful pillars and daring airy arches. The great Bavarian architects of the eighteenth century were masters of the use of light. To walk into the church of Oberammergau and turn to look back at the double organ chamber and choir loft is to see gilded, delicate carving and moulding illuminated with almost miraculous shafts of light from concealed win-

(*top*) Hans Schwaighofer
as Judas in 1950, and (*below*)
Judas betrays Jesus (Anton
Preisinger) with a kiss

dows. Yet the double loft seems in fact a treble loft, for Schmuzer painted a 'three-dimensional' canopy, covering a painted altar bearing seven candlesticks, to rise, over steps it seems, from the uppermost pipes of the organ.

Such an architect attracted brilliant disciples. Schmuzer brought to Oberammergau a young painter named Matthäus Günther, to whom he entrusted the great dome over the church of St Peter and St Paul. Here in 1741 Günther depicted the martyrdom of these two patron saints and their entry into the heavenly city. Schmuzer reserved for himself the painting of the choir, where in 1761 he completed the great fresco of Mary as queen of the holy rosary. He was also shrewd enough to employ the *Lüftlmaler* himself – Franz Zwinck – to create the illusion of still more airy balustrades inside the parish church.

At work in Bavaria at this time was a sculptor of remarkable gifts named Franz Xavier Schmädl. Schmädl was an artist of almost playful piety, renowned above all for his delightfully human cherubs and *putti*. Joseph Schmuzer employed him to create the great altar of the parish church, and also the no less brilliant side altars. The great altar, which Schmädl finished in the year 1762, has a huge and yet delicate free-standing canopy, rising on six pillars and topped by a carved 'curtain'. On either side, as well as the two patron saints of the church, stand St Joseph and St Joachim, sculpted in white with golden haloes. Holding up the canopy and curtain are no fewer than twenty-five cherubs, and another couple seem to be sliding up and down the two outside pillars.

On the north side of the church Schmädl created an altar dedicated to the Holy Trinity. The villagers asked him to include a statue of St Gregory Thaumaturgos, who was considered especially good at preventing floods, since at this time the river Ammer frequently burst its banks. On the south side, Schmädl made an altar in honour of St Anthony – another homely touch since, among other virtues, St Anthony was considered the patron saint of pigs. Flanking Anthony, Schmädl set statues of St Francis of Assisi and his co-worker St Clare (a sign, perhaps, of the Italian influence on these great rococo artists).

The whole church could have been created only at this precise moment in the eighteenth century. (On the northside-altar one of the saints wears delightful eighteenth-century lace-up boots!) Although it is Schmuzer's masterpiece, his genius allowed Matthäus Günther, Franz Zwinck and Franz Xaver Schmädl to share his triumph. Every detail is brilliant: on the font-cover the Baptist baptizes Jesus; Schmädl's tremendous pulpit is topped by an angel, announcing the Word of God by blowing a golden trumpet. And yet the church of St Peter and St Paul, Oberammergau, remains a village church, albeit a most remarkable one. On the west wall, underneath the choir loft, is a touching memorial, done not by one of these great rococo artists but by an unknown villager. It commemorates the wars of the early nineteenth century, when twelve Oberammergauers went to fight in Russia and only three returned. Two obelisks honour the village's dead sons. A woman in traditional costume weeps. And a repulsive skeleton dances with glee.

Here the Oberammergauers rejoiced, were baptized, were married and

Judas (Hans Zwinck) off-stage

buried their dead. In the graveyard lie two of the village's greatest sons. On the south side is the readily recognized memorial to Pastor Alois Daisenberger, to whom the Passion Play owes its present form. He died in 1883. His memorial carries a bust by Professor Otto Lang of Munich, who was born in Oberammergau. On one side is the legend '*Seine Werke folgen ihm nach*' ('His works survive him'); on the other, '*Sein Vorbild sei uns heilig*' ('Let us keep his ideal holy'). And on the north side of the parish church is the tomb of Rochus Dedler, the schoolmaster who created the music for the Passion Play, 'erected' (as its legend announces) 'by friends and pupils in memory of our unforgettable teacher'.

Even out of season, so to speak, it is thus impossible in Oberammergau to escape the impact of the famous Passion Play. The Corpus Christi procession from church to theatre is a symbol of the fact that today the village has two spiritual centres, church and theatre, intimately bound together.

When no Passion Play is being performed the visitor has the privilege of going backstage in the theatre. Here are exhibited costumes over a hundred years old, as well as those used in the play today, the finest of them made of oriental cloth. To see how the costumes have moved towards greater historical accuracy in their detail is fascinating. Backstage, too, are rows and rows of armour, spears and swords, all made in Oberammergau, some of them used in half a dozen or more productions of the play. On the walls are photographs of previous productions of the play, staged in these costumes. The subtle blending of colours in the great crowd scenes is impressive – though after so many years' devotion to the Passion Play the villagers of Oberammergau might be expected to have a sure instinct for such matters.

Because the acoustics of the theatre are perfect, the only concession to modernity is the use of loudspeakers to call the actors from their dressing-rooms to the stage. These rooms are surprisingly modest. That of the actor playing Jesus has a small wash-basin. Carefully laid out along with his robes are crowns of thorns, once woven from local thorns and now – in the pursuit of greater and greater realism – woven from thorns from the Holy Land.

To stand on the great stage itself is even more impressive. Permanently on display there is the heavier of the two crosses used in the play, the one on which Jesus is crucified. (The one he carries to Calvary, though resembling the other, is lighter, being hollowed out.) The heavier cross weighs over 300 lb and the visitor can examine at close quarters the almost impossibly tiny hollows where, for just under half an hour, the actor playing Jesus must balance his feet as he hangs on the cross. On stage are displayed the two-hundred-year-old table and stools used during the portrayal of the Last Supper. And to one side is the cage where in the Temple scene are kept the doves.

By any standards the stage at Oberammergau is a remarkable theatrical construction. The whole is over forty metres wide and forty metres deep, and one section of it can be lowered and raised to ease scenery changes. The forestage holds not only the Prologue, with his forty-eight-strong choir, but also, in crowd scenes, over 800 actors. Over the proscenium

Casting the play,
11 November 1949;
the election committee
at work

the flies are electrically operated, again to speed the thirty-three changes
of scenery. Speed is essential; without it the play, which nowadays lasts
five and a half hours (from 9 to 11.30 in the morning and from 2.30 to
5.30 in the afternoon) would be intolerably long.

Even out of season the visitor emerges from the peace of the Passion
Play theatre into a busy, bustling village. In the square is a modest
modern statue of Jesus riding into Jerusalem on an ass – the scene which
starts the action of the play. He carries his own palm branch in one hand
and blesses the crowd with the other. The rock below the statue is a
fountain. Somehow that statue and fountain suggest the peace and blessing of this Bavarian village, no matter how busy and occupied its streets.
The impact of the Passion Play is such that Oberammergau could never
be just another tourist village.

8 The Country around Oberammergau

On the north side of the Kofel, on the Maxiersteig path, is a remarkable and huge statue of the crucified Jesus, surrounded by his mother and closest disciples. It was given to the people of Oberammergau by King Ludwig I I of Bavaria after that solitary brooding monarch had watched a performance of the Passion Play in 1871 entirely alone. Ludwig chose its site. He wrote its inscription: 'To the people of Oberammergau, devoted to art and faithful to the ways of their fathers.'

The subject of a crucifixion is intrinsically tragic. This particular sculpture has two other tragic associations. The massive pieces of Kelheim marble were sculpted in the workshops of Professor Halbig of Munich and by 1875 were ready to be transported to Oberammergau. Altogether the group was to tower thirty-nine feet over the roadway. The socket for the cross alone weighed 480 hundredweight. The steam-locomotive pulling it over the pass from Oberau to Oberammergau gave up the struggle, and the socket had to be pulled laboriously along by eighty firemen and a hundred horses in relays. In an attempt to avoid a repetition of this problem, a special carriage was built to carry the statue of St John to Oberammergau. Halfway there the carriage overturned. The statue fell on and killed a master stonemason named Hauser and then rolled over, crushing to death a stone-cutter named Kofelenz.

Nevertheless the great crucifixion group was at last assembled and consecrated on the birthday of Queen Marie Friederike, the king's widowed mother. Here lies the third tragic aspect of the sculpture. Each year on the anniversary of its consecration King Ludwig would arrive at its foot to pray for his mother and his younger brother Otto. But in fact, Ludwig hated his mother. 'I shall never cease to revere her because she has the honour of being mother of the king,' he once declared. 'But there are times when she overdoes the mother and underplays the king. I am the sovereign; she is simply my mother and at the same time my subject.' Otto had gone insane at the age of twenty-one. The Bavarian royal family had a history of insanity; but Otto's decline could partly be attributed to some of the treatment meted out to him by his elder brother. Once when they were playing together Ludwig had tied up the younger boy and threatened to behead him, and if a courtier had not suddenly appeared he might have succeeded. Ludwig himself showed signs of incipient madness as a child. He loved to dress up as a nun; he gave away most of his money; he grew so much attached to a pet tortoise that it had to be taken from him. He never learned to love human beings much. And finally he went insane himself. The cruelty with which he had treated Otto he applied also to royal servants. He would kick and beat them for what in his eyes was the slightest error. At other times he would have the heads of offending menials banged against the wall, and then force them to kneel, head on the ground, until he gave them permission to rise. A characteristic example – though a minor one – of Ludwig's bizarre behaviour occurred after he had seen the Passion Play of 1871. Delighted with the performance, he invited the leading actors to his nearby palace of Linderhof. To each he gave a valuable silver spoon, save for Judas, who was given a tin one.

Eventually the king's behaviour (and his profligacy) proved intolerable. In 1886 he was deposed and placed under arrest in Berg Castle on the banks of the Starnberg lake. On the evening of Whit Sunday, 13 June, Ludwig and his physician, Dr Bernhard von Gudden, went for a walk, wearing overcoats and carrying umbrellas because a storm was brewing. That same evening their drowned bodies were found floating in the water. Von Gudden, whose eye was blackened, may well have tried to restrain Ludwig either from trying to escape or from committing suicide. The king's overcoat and jacket were found floating separately from his body.

Yet along with Ludwig's madness went genius. As a child he loved to build churches and monasteries with toy bricks. And no one who visits Oberammergau today should miss visiting at least some of the astonishing castles close by, for which the extraordinary genius of Ludwig II was responsible.

The only one to be completed, Schloss Linderhof, lies a few kilometres south of Oberammergau. Here Ludwig lived for eight years of his life, imagining himself as the true successor of the French 'Sun King', Louis XIV. Since Louis XIV had declared '*L'état c'est moi*', Ludwig called his Schloss, in an anagram, 'Meicost Ettal'. He instructed his architect, Georg Dollmann, to build a small château in the style of Louis XIV's Trianon at Versailles. Dollmann's designs were charming, richly ornate and brilliant. Ludwig was not always satisfied. True to his Bavarian origins, on several ceilings Dollmann wished to portray gods and goddesses with rococo brilliance, combining a protruding stucco leg or piece of clothing with an apparently 'three-dimensional' roof painting. Wherever this was achieved, Ludwig objected. 'His Majesty does not approve of the figures on the ceiling of this room having feet in relief,' he complained in 1872. 'The gods too should not have been modelled but simply painted on the ceiling.' Fortunately Dollmann sometimes got his own way.

But Linderhof mostly reflects both the genius and the waywardness of the king. Everywhere are peacocks, for he hated flags (as symbolizing war) and preferred the gorgeously plumed bird as his emblem. Linderhof contains marble from countless countries. Sèvres porcelain, treasures from China, a chandelier in Indian ivory and an intricate hall of mirrors combine with gilding, needlework and painting to create a sumptuous yet small-scale palace.

Everywhere is the influence of the Sun King. His statue is in the entrance hall and overhead is his motto, embossed on the ceiling: *Nec pluribus impar*. Ludwig's bedchamber, looking out on to a long terrace with a cascade of water falling down to a Neptune fountain, was to be a worthy successor to those of Versailles.

The gardens themselves, laid out by Karl Effner, are both romantic and formal, with ornamental flowerbeds in the shape of Bourbon lilies, a fountain 105 feet high, and statues of dolphins, Venus and Marie Antoinette. The western parterre has a life-size bust of Louis XIV and the eastern parterre one of Louis XVI of France. Ludwig bought a remarkable Moorish kiosk from the Berlin railway magnate B.H. Strousberg and erected it in the garden. There, too, he constructed an amazing 'Venus Grotto' containing artificial stalagmites and stalactites illuminated in many different colours, with an underground lake and scenes simulating the first act of Richard Wagner's 'Tannhäuser'.

In its magnificence Schloss Linderhof also reveals something of Ludwig's madness. Everywhere in the hall of mirrors are bizarrely set the vases he collected so obsessively. He preferred objects to people. Schloss Linderhof contains one of his celebrated 'Tischlein-deck'-dich' – a table set over a trapdoor. When the king pulled a bell, his servants cranked the table down and speedily set it with food and drink, cranking it up again so that he could eat alone without even seeing his menials. After 1880 he almost invariably dined alone when at Linderhof, accompanied only by the busts of Marie Antoinette and Louis XIV, saying that they came only when he bade them and left just as quickly.

As the king's mania increased, his courtiers found it more and more difficult to deal with this aspect of his withdrawn personality. At the last moment he would cancel a royal dinner-party, when all the guests had been invited and the protocol carefully arranged. If he did have to dine in public as part of his duties, he would describe it as 'mounting the scaffold' and drink up to ten glasses of champagne beforehand to give himself Dutch courage. It is odd that this insane, sometimes sadistic man should have managed to create at Schloss Linderhof a building so enchanting. Obviously inspired by Versailles, it manages to retain an intimacy in all its sumptuously decorated and furnished rooms which Versailles never achieved.

If Linderhof displays Ludwig II's obsession with seventeenth- and eighteenth-century French royalty, not far away another extraordinary castle which he built reveals his passion for one of his most remarkable contemporaries: the composer Richard Wagner. Ludwig became fascinated by Wagner at the age of thirteen and when in 1861 he heard his first Wagner opera (which was 'Lohengrin'), fascination turned into obsession. His obsession undoubtedly helped Wagner. Less than five weeks after becoming king, Ludwig sought out the composer, who was in hiding, desperate to avoid his many creditors. The two men were entranced with each other. 'The king understands me like my own soul,' wrote Wagner. 'Rest assured that I shall do everything possible to make up for what you have suffered in the past,' Ludwig promised. 'I shall banish from you for ever the petty cares of everyday life and give you the peace you have longed for, to let you spread the mighty wings of your genius.' The revolutionary composer was in fact seen by many as a dangerous influence on the king and in 1865 the two men were forced to part, but not before Ludwig had paid Wagner's debts, made him comparatively rich and given enormous support to his work. Wagner himself spoke at times almost as if his music was the outcome of some kind of collaboration with his patron. 'Long after we are dead,' he wrote, 'our work will continue to delight and dazzle the centuries.' For his part, Ludwig set about immortalizing the composer in his fairytale castle, the remarkable Schloss Neuschwanstein.

To drive to Neuschwanstein from Schloss Linderhof is a matter of little more than forty kilometres. The route towards Füssen leads by the romantic Plansee through St Ulrich's country, from whose Augsburg monastery the Oberammergauers took their first version of the Passion Play. (There is *en route* a small chapel to St Ulrich, and even St Ulrich's bridge four kilometres south of Füssen, with an Ulrichsbrücke guesthouse.) Travellers need their passports, since the route leads in and out of Austria.

Signposts from Füssen do not read 'Neuschwanstein' but 'Königsschlösser', since there are in fact two astonishing castles on the same site near Schwangau. Both suddenly appear, perched high up on the mountainside. To the left is Neuschwanstein, gleaming white. High on the right is Hohenschwangau, pale yellow and brick red, with its turrets and crenellations, surmounted by a white swan.

Here the young Ludwig was brought up. The twelfth-century knights of Schwangau had built a castle on this spot which Napoleon virtually destroyed. Hohenschwangau was re-created by Ludwig's father. Here the inspiration is not the French Sun King and Versailles, but a dream of the Middle Ages. Gothic tracery, coats of arms, suits of armour, 'medieval' stained glass, triptychs and paintings from the Middle Ages give the Schloss its character. Legends of the Swan Knights, painted between 1832 and 1834, adorn the dining-room. Other rooms have wall-paintings depicting the achievements of Charlemagne. In the great hall built for Ludwig's mother, scenes from the lives of women in the Middle Ages cover the walls: they hunt with falcons, play the harp, read to children – as Queen Marie Friederike herself never did. This hall contains a huge chandelier, made of silver and decorated with swans. Everywhere are reminders of the old heroes of Germany (including Martin Luther). In one room is a statue of Charles Martel killing one of his enemies. In another is painted the Saga of Theodoric, King of the Ostrogoths. On the walls of one room King Authari of the Langobards woos his bride, Princess Theodelinde. The centrepiece of the massive table in the 'Hall of the Heroes' is a huge gilded bronze depicting the Nibelungen saga.

Interspersed among all this is evidence of the daily lives of the young Ludwig and his family. Nineteenth-century *Kachelöfen*, tiled in the Gothic style, warmed the rooms. At odds with the rest of the Schloss is Queen Marie Friederike's bedroom, decorated in the oriental style with settees presented by Sultan Muhammed II, after Crown Prince Maximilian's visit to Turkey in 1833. On the way in to the Queen's chapel are photographs of her sons Ludwig and Otto, both with strange wild eyes.

Here Wagner stayed with Ludwig. Here is Wagner's piano. A bust of the composer stands next to a gilt-framed picture of Ludwig as a

Knight of St George. Here the king was inspired to build Neuschwanstein.

'I intend to rebuild the ancient ruined castle of Hohenschwangau in the true style of a castle of the old German knights,' Ludwig told Wagner in 1868. He completed only fifteen out of sixty-five projected rooms and halls, but what he did achieve is astonishing. The ruins of an old watchtower were demolished and part of a mountain peak was blasted away to provide a base for the new Schloss. At first the rooms were built in the Gothic style. Ludwig's bedroom has a canopy over the spot where he planned to sleep that resembles the canopies over medieval tombs. Its *Kachelöfen* has Gothic tiling and statues at each corner. On one side of the bed, running water poured from a swan's beak when he wished to wash. On the other side is a prayer-stool with holy pictures to inspire the king's devotions. And leading off this bedroom is a small private chapel, also in the 'medieval' Gothic style. Julius Hofmann of Munich designed the altarpiece, with its carved triptych. A stained-glass window by the Munich glass-maker Mayr shows King Louis the Holy of France receiving the viaticum.

The rest of Neuschwanstein is built in Romanesque and Byzantine style. For seventeen years builders and artists (over a hundred painters and fourteen wood-carvers) laboured to create it. All work stopped on the king's death. Ludwig's Byzantine throne-room never received its throne. Today it resembles a Byzantine basilica, with an inlaid marble floor (of over two and a half million small pieces), plaster pillars painted to represent marble, galleries for courtiers who in the end never came to an audience, a huge golden chandelier and golden walls, with pictures of saints between palm trees.

Yet all is as fresh today as it was over a hundred years ago. The repeated painted patterns of the great winding staircases are as bold as ever. The intricate metalwork of the doors and the hanging lamps has not tarnished. The balconies and vistas are breathtaking. The kitchens are remarkable for their engineering brilliance, with piped water and hot air vents, with spits driven by turbines to a design of Leonardo da Vinci but perfected in the nineteenth century. Ludwig conceived an ancient Schloss constructed with all the modern skills of the industrial revolution. Indeed the finest view of Neuschwanstein is from the bridge dedicated to Ludwig's mother, a frightening ironwork span across the Poellat waterfall, 304 feet above the ground, built in 1866 by brilliant Munich engineers.

Above all, Schloss Neuschwanstein celebrates Richard Wagner. Off the king's living-room is yet another fake 'Venus Grotto' similar to that at Schloss Linderhof but this time incorporated into the castle itself. Everywhere are scenes from the great operas. In Ludwig's study Tannhäuser is depicted in the Venusberg, as well as at the singers' contest and playing for a dance. The king's living-room is decorated with the Lohengrin saga and scenes from 'Tristan and Isolde'. The singers' contest reappears in the king's dining-room, and 'Tristan and Isolde' in the bedroom. And for Wagner Ludwig had built on the fifth floor of Schloss Neuschwanstein a magnificent Singers' Hall, decorated with scenes from 'Parzifal', with stage designs incorporating Klingsor's magic forest. The Singers' Hall at Neuschwanstein is acoustically perfect. It was never used either in Wagner's lifetime or in Ludwig's.

To gain some insight into the strange genius of Ludwig I I of Bavaria, the visitor would have to travel a couple of hours or so from Oberammergau to Bavaria's largest lake, the Chiemsee, where the king built his third great Schloss, Herrenchiemsee. But at Neuschwanstein, so near the town of Füssen, the visitor would be foolish not to pause for a moment to look at the treasures of that town. Füssen is a town of tall old houses and narrow charming streets. Here in the eighth or ninth century was founded the Benedictine monastery of St Magnus. Its eighteenth-century cloister is white and cool, with an apparently 'three-dimensional' balcony and pillars painted on one side. The monastery church was originally a Romanesque basilica, and some old wall-paintings from that time have recently been discovered by archaeologists working there. But between 1700 and 1717 the baroque architect Jakob Herkomer transformed the interior, adding a fantastically carved altar and organ loft, as well as delightfully early rococo pews. In the middle of the eighteenth century Herkomer's great-nephew, Franz Karl Fischer, designed and decorated the pink and red church of the Holy Spirit, which stands outside the monastery.

And near Füssen are two of the most remarkable churches in the whole of Germany. The route is by way of Steingaden. On the right just north of Füssen is the lovely white plasterwork of the pilgrims' church of St Coloman – not one of the two great churches, but still worth a visit, partly because it affords another fine view of both Schloss Hohenschwangau and Schloss Neuschwanstein and partly because it once again reminds us of the great plague which was responsible for the vow of Oberammergau. St Coloman was reputed to be particularly skilled at protecting the faithful from the plague. He also cared for cattle, and on his feast day (13 October) animals are still blessed in his name at Hohenschwangau. Inside his tiny pilgrims' church are simple pictures of the saint himself blessing cattle, some of which are drawn twice as large as their owners.

At Steingaden a right turn towards Oberammergau leads shortly to the signs pointing to what is probably the greatest rococo church in Europe, the Wieskirche. If the finest baroque churches are frequently in the smallest Bavarian villages, Wies transcends this rule by standing all by itself in a meadow. The site was miraculously determined. In 1730 the monks of Steingaden carved a statue of the scourged Christ to use in their Good Friday procession. They were inspired by a vision of the Blessed Crescentia of Kaufbeuren, who in the early eighteenth century persuaded many in Bavaria to adore the Jesus who had thus suffered. But a few years later the monks decided that their statue was 'too intense' in its depiction of the incident in Jesus's passion, and they threw the statue out. It was rescued by a farmer's pious wife named Maria Lory, who built a small chapel for it near her own home in the meadow. On 14 June 1738, as she prayed before the figure, she perceived that it was weeping.

The miracle persuaded the monks of Steingaden that they had been foolish to discard their statue. Pilgrims came in such droves to see the statue and pray before the scourged Christ that soon the little chapel in the meadow was too small to contain them. The architect Dominikus Zimmermann was commissioned to build a new one.

Zimmermann had settled in Füssen in 1708, moving to Landsberg on the Lech eight years later, where he was elected mayor. After completing his masterpiece, the Wieskirche, he built himself a small house near it and lived there until he died.

The exterior of the Wieskirche is deliberately gentle and muted, painted in pale yellow and white, its roof-line deliberately shaped to mirror the line of the mountains behind. Inside it is a riot of pink and blue, gold leaf, green and red. The high altar was finished in 1749, and the image of the scourged Christ was solemnly taken there from its home in the little church. Six blue-veined columns on either side of the choir lead the eye to four red-veined columns carrying the canopy over this high altar, which in turn is topped by a scene of the heavenly Jerusalem, where a silver Lamb of God stands on a silver book with seven silver seals.

Dominikus Zimmermann employed his brilliant brother, Johann Baptist Zimmermann, to create many of the fine frescoes and stucco designs inside the Wieskirche. The ceiling fresco of the nave shows the Last Judgment; but Johann Baptist Zimmermann refused to portray a stern and condemning Jesus. Instead he shows Christ the good shepherd, lovingly forgiving and welcoming back his erring flock. His Last Judgment is not a day of wrath but one of joy.

The nave of the Wieskirche is oval in design. Then, at its four 'corners', Dominikus Zimmermann placed huge white flamboyant statues of the four Latin doctors of the church: St Ambrose, with a golden beehive, crozier and mitre; St Augustine, mitred like Ambrose, with a golden flame of inspiration coming from his breast; St Jerome, in a cardinal's golden hat; and St Gregory the Great, wearing the golden papal tiara. Each carries a golden Bible. On Jerome's Bible is a golden skull. In the organ loft Zimmermann set a gold and white organ with silver-gilt pipes, surmounted by a pelican feeding her young with her own body. And then, brilliantly concealing his artifice, he used woodwork covered in stucco to create the illusion of arches which seem to fly upside-down and yet do not fall. As a final *jeu d'esprit*, he placed on his rich pulpit, with its awesome eye of God and flames of the Holy Spirit, four delightful cherubs dressed as St Ambrose, St Augustine, St Jerome and St Gregory the Great.

This same devout playfulness is displayed in the second great church of the area, that of the Rottenbuch monastery on the Munich road from Wies. The artists were not, however, the Zimmermann brothers but Joseph Schmuzer and Franz Xaver Schmädl who created the great church at Oberammergau. Schmuzer travelled and worked as far away as Moravia; but nothing he created is more impressive than the churches of Rottenbuch and Oberammergau. If anything, Rottenbuch is the more riotous in its colours and invention. The pulpit alone is a masterpiece. Here again is the awesome eye of God. Over the globe an angel holds the Ten Commandments. Two fat cherubs blow golden horns to announce

The river Ammer, from which both Oberammergau and its sister village Unterammergau take their names

the Word of God. Supporting the pulpit are St John with his eagle, quill pen poised over his Gospel, and St Matthew with his bull, overcome with rapture. The organ is delicately set into its gallery, with a pink marble arch holding up a smaller choir organ. On either side of the long canopied apse, Schmädl has set cherubs who play the fiddle, flugelhorns and kettle-drums, while one of them sings from a golden sheet of music.

The road from Steingaden to Oberammergau runs through its smaller sister-village, Unterammergau. Here too, among a number of charming eating-places and *Gaststätten*, is another beautiful church. After the Thirty Years' War, St Nicholas church at Unterammergau was unusable, but by the end of the seventeenth century only a new tower had been constructed. Finally in 1709 a new baroque church was begun. The church of St Nicholas is far less ornate than the parish church of Oberammergau, but its frescoes are delicate, and its high altar (again by Schmädl) is fine and impressive. Not to be missed is the chapel of the Holy Blood. The altar on the south side of the nave has a charming picture of the martyrdom of St Veit. While soldiers apply a light to the wood around the naked saint, a cherub above him holds out his heavenly crown.

The visitor who has time to spare needs a day or so to explore Ludwig's third great castle, Herrenchiemsee. If Schloss Linderhof represents Ludwig's version of the Trianon at Versailles, Herrenchiemsee is Versailles itself. But he slept there, in all, only twenty-three times.

To reach Herrenchiemsee is in itself a pleasure since the island of Herreninsel is accessible only by a leisurely motor-boat trip through the yachts of the Chiemsee. A gentle walk through the forest reveals the

Bavarian king's reconstruction of the garden approach to Versailles, with its statuary and fountains. Wide, low steps lead up to the long pale-yellow Schloss, three storeys high, topped with armour and flaming urns. Inside, instead of copying Versailles, Ludwig re-created it with the aid of the nineteenth-century scientific revolution, so that for instance the huge staircase (modelled on the ambassadors' staircase of Versailles which was demolished in 1752), as well as incorporating eighteen different kinds of marble, includes a modern glass roof. Although the peace-loving Ludwig filled Herrenchiemsee with reproductions of his favourite symbol, the peacock, he also saw fit to include ceiling frescoes dedicated to Mars, the god of war. His sumptuous bedroom, patterned on that in which the eighteenth-century kings of France received supplicants and courtiers, displays the symbol of the Sun King over the bed. Scenes from the life of Louis XIV cover the walls of the main ante-chamber. The next ante-chamber has windows modelled on the famous 'bull's eye' windows of Versailles, and in the centre is an equestrian statue of Louis XIV. The state room has a ceiling fresco fittingly depicting Mercury, the bringer of news. Meissen porcelain lends opulence to every spare corner of Herrenchiemsee. Ludwig's study, which he used so seldom, is dominated by a portrait of Louis XV of France, and his working desk is modelled on one designed for that king in the 1760s. But the most stupendous homage paid by Ludwig II to the kings of France is the colossal reproduction in Herrenchiemsee of the Versailles Hall of Mirrors. Ninety-eight metres long, Ludwig's hall of mirrors is lit by chandeliers and twenty-four candelabra on either side (holding altogether 5,680 candles).

The castle was never finished. Bare brick still awaits its marble covering where the second great staircase leads down to Ludwig's huge circular bath. On this staircase stands a statue of the doomed king, worked in marble in 1870 by the sculptor Elizabeth Ney. And underneath the royal dining-room can still be seen the actual mechanism for working yet another 'Tischlein-deck'-dich' which he installed so as to avoid too close a contact with the human race.

The return route to Oberammergau brings the imagination back to the Passion Play. The motorway which runs south from Munich passes within 500 metres of Eschenlohe, whence Kaspar Schisler brought the plague. Then the road turns north to Ettal, four kilometres from Oberammergau. The Benedictine monks who were driven from Ettal in 1803 and died in a 'secularized' world were replaced in 1900 by members of the same order. Today Ettal is a monastery which also provides the neighbourhood with a parish church. The old church founded by Ludwig the Bavarian in 1370 had been an unusual twelve-angled building. In 1710 a start was made on the new west front, and then a choir was added. The choir, the library and most of the abbey were ravaged by a fire in 1744; 30,000 books were destroyed, although the precious statue of the Virgin Mary brought by Ludwig from Italy was saved and can still be seen at Ettal.

To rebuild their abbey church in 1744 the monks of Ettal employed the favourite architect of the Elector of Bavaria, Enrico Zuccalli. Zuccalli, an Italian, kept the original twelve-angled plan of Ettal and clothed it in

A mid-nineteenth-century cartoonist caricatures the Oberammergauers

magnificent rococo. But in place of the old Gothic spire he designed a gigantic cupola, forty metres in height, topped by a lantern over fifty metres high. He employed artists of genius to work on the interior of his new church, where the only straight lines are those of the floor and walls. Inside everything is astonishingly irregular and yet it coheres perfectly. In 1751 and 1752 the artist J.J. Zeiller painted over 400 figures on the ceiling of the rotunda, depicting the glories of St Benedict and his monastic order. Josef Lindner, a master stone-cutter from Salzburg, made the frame of the high altar which now houses the Italian statue of the Virgin Mary. Six side-altars were designed by the architect Johann Baptist Straub, who also made the Bavarian rococo pulpit. A great chandelier hangs in the centre of Ettal church. The four confessionals are surrounded by cherubs and angels. The tracery of the organ case on its delicate pink and white balcony is complemented by that of the two theatre-like 'boxes' which seem to cling magically to the north and south walls. Asymmetrical shields, cartouches, swags, urns and picture frames contribute to the ecstatic mood of the building.

Yet this light and airy church also speaks of the discipline and sacrifice of the Christian faith. On the altar of the Blessed Sacrament, Zeiller depicted St Corbinian condemning his lord, Duke Grimoald, for profaning the sacrament of marriage by taking a concubine. And another altar shows St Catherine of Alexandria about to be beheaded in a marketplace, while angels wait to bear her to heaven.

Ettal is a living monastery and a living church. The life of a monk in the Middle Ages survives here into the twentieth century. Outside, the visitor can still buy the original 'Ettalerklosterliqueur'. The monks still process in the village and in their cloisters, decorating their church with branches of trees, on the great feast-days of the church. And as we have seen, their piety and learning are still available whenever the villagers of Oberammergau seek to adapt their Passion Play to the needs of a new age.

9 Today and Tomorrow

Oberammergau changes slowly. The drama critic who reported on the Passion Play season of 1950 for *The Times* had been present at a performance in 1934. Sixteen years and a bitter war had come between those performances. Yet he felt he had come back to an unchanged village, with its broad meadowlands still closed in on every side by mountains symbolizing the natural seclusion of 'a peculiar community ... fashioned by a history and tradition that the outer world cannot share'. The Oberammergauers who today put bells round the necks of their cattle, and at Epiphany chalk on their doors the initials of Kaspar, Melchior and Balthasar – the three kings who worshipped the infant Christ – are still following the ancient traditions of their Bavarian forefathers.

Since their solemn vow three hundred and fifty years ago the Passion Play has become the central part of the tradition of Oberammergau. The account-books kept by the village in the nineteenth century show them buying the costumes of the passion plays of neighbouring villages – Kohlgrub, Mittelwald, and so on – as these plays were abandoned. At Oberammergau the play has gone from strength to strength. Earlier generations laboured and today's generation enters into their labours.

A tradition is not something dead. Traditions grow and develop. But even when they have modified their play, the Oberammergauers have consciously respected what has gone before. On 23 April 1883, Burgermeister Lang put this succinctly at the funeral service of Alois Daisen-

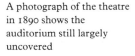

A photograph of the theatre in 1890 shows the auditorium still largely uncovered

berger, who as much as anyone was responsible for the text as it is performed today: 'Respecting tradition, his skilful pen refined the text, and enabled us to come into the inheritance of our forefathers.'

But what began as a small Bavarian village re-enacting the passion of Jesus as a thanksgiving for its deliverance from the plague has been transformed into a huge tourist attraction. The process started in the early nineteenth century, after the hostility of the Electors of Bavaria had been transformed into enthusiastic royal patronage. Many have asked whether the traditional pieties of Oberammergau will not one day be swamped by the demands of commercialism.

(*top*) Joseph Mayr as Jesus, a photograph of 1890, and (*below*) Anton Preisinger in the performance of 1950

The Oberammergauers have always insisted that they are presenting an act of worship quite as much as a play. Alois Daisenberger once warned his fellow-villagers that 'if selfish reasons, if the mere desire for fame and gain were to inspire our actions, no blessing will rest upon them'. Whenever they have consented to be interviewed (and Oberammergauers have often been reluctant to agree to this), actors and actresses in the Passion Play invariably reveal that they understand this. Hansi Preisinger, who played Mary Magdalene in 1930, said: 'The Oberammergauer does not feel as if he were acting in a theatre; to us the play means keeping the sacred vow of our forefathers.' The play is a means of proclaiming the Gospel. Anni Rutz, elected to play the Virgin Mary in 1930, said: 'I am glad to be permitted to contribute my share to the mission of the Oberammergauers.'

No doubt the Oberammergauers who watched the play felt this when it was performed in the early years in their parish church. But audiences have continued to feel it, even when they have been drawn from other lands and have watched the play while seated in an auditorium. Hans Christian Andersen came from Denmark to Oberammergau and observed that to see the entire play was like going to a church where no priest merely stood up and preached. He called the performance a 'celebration'. Ninety years later the drama critic of *The Times* declared: 'Audiences do not go to the Passion to criticize the production or the acting. However interesting as an art form, it remains essentially a religious service.'

From time to time visitors have prophesied that this cannot last. In 1910 the American scholar Montrose J. Moses wrote: 'Time alone will tell whether the communal ideal and whether the communal mission, which guard the minds of 2,000 Bavarian peasants, will be able in isolated reverence to withstand the suffusing forces of civilization.' He hoped that their ideal and the spirit of mission could withstand commercialism and the outside world, but he feared that 'every decade opens the sluices ... the building of the new theatre for the production of 1900 is part example of how time and circumstance work against tradition.' (Hans Andersen would have disagreed. In 1860 he sat in the open-air auditorium in the rain. No one opened an umbrella for fear of obscuring the view of those sitting behind!)

Of course Oberammergau has never been exempt from the economic problems which face the rest of the world. The introduction to the programme of 1922 starkly observes that the villagers would have put on

Second Edition.

PROGRAMME OF ARRANGEMENTS

FOR

OBER AMMERGAU

AVAILABLE FOR ONE OR MORE PASSENGERS
BY ANY ROUTE, ANY DAY,

INCLUDING

. . The Bavarian Highlands, . .

The Dolomite and Salzkammergut Districts,

The Tyrol, and

All Parts of Central Europe.

WITH MAP OF OBER AMMERGAU DISTRICT.

Under the personal contracts and management of

THOS. COOK & SON,

Official Agents of the Passion Play Committee.

Originators of the European Tourist and Excursion System—Established 1841.

Specially appointed Passenger Agents to the Royal British Commission for the Vienna Exhibition, 1873, Philadelphia, 1876, Paris, 1878, Colonial and Indian, 1886, Chicago, 1893, and Paris, 1900; also specially appointed Agents for the Antwerp Exhibition, 1894, Amsterdam, 1895, Brussels, 1897, Stockholm, 1897; also Sole Passenger Agents for the Vienna Jubilee Exhibition, 1898, for England, France, and the United States of America; the St. Louis Exhibition, 1904; the Milan Exhibition, 1906; and for the Dublin Exhibition, 1907; also Official Passenger Agents for the International Exhibition, Christchurch, New Zealand, 1906 to 1907; Franco-British Exhibition, London, 1908; also Official Agents of the Passion Play Committee, Ober Ammergau, 1910.

Chief Office—LUDGATE CIRCUS, LONDON.

Chief American Office—245, Broadway, New York.

THOS. COOK & SON LTD
30 APR 1971

The rise of group travel:
Thomas Cook's brochures
for 1910 and 1984

their play in 1920 but for the political and economic problems of their country and the need to cope with the victims of the Great War. And the solvency of Oberammergau in 1950 absolutely depended on the success of the Passion Play. But tourism also seemed to threaten what was precious and unique to the mountain village. 'It may be true that the tourist traffic contributed a lot to improve the financial situation of these people,' conceded Hermine Diemer (who had married into

INTER CHURCH TRAVEL

INTER CHURCH TRAVEL

Oberammergau 1984

350th Anniversary

MAY TO SEPTEMBER 1984

(*above*) The interior of the theatre basically as it is today, designed by Karl Lautenschlager of the Munich Court Theatre in 1899. Thomas Cook's brochure described this advanced design unkindly (but accurately) as being 'roughly like an airport shed'

(*right*) Backstage the flies are painted – by old-fashioned brush and by spray-gun. This photograph shows the preparations for the performance of 1950, which demanded much post-war repair of the Passion Play theatre

Oberammergau) in 1930; 'to their souls and minds, however, it worked out to be harmful rather than beneficial.'

This was a premature judgement. The Passion Play and those who take part in it have not been led astray by the outside world. The man who played Jesus in 1950, Anton Preisinger, was sent by his parents to board at a school thirty miles from Oberammergau. He ran away, arriving back home in the small hours of the morning, and thereupon he made his parents promise that he could leave the school and be brought up in his home village. As an adult, apart from his war service, he remained content to stay there. He played an angel in the year Hermine Diemer made her gloomy observation, and Lazarus in 1934. He was asked to play Jesus a second time in 1960, and for the rest of the time he ran the Alte Post Hotel. The Passion Play of Oberammergau is still powerful enough to dominate and fulfil the lives of many of its villagers.

Part of the strength of the play, for Protestant and Catholic alike, is its biblical foundation. Like many before and since, Hans Andersen believed he was watching 'the last remains, in our time, of the Middle Ages'. But the play has long since ceased to be a mere survival of the past, in the fashion of, say, the Chester or York cycle of mystery plays – fascinating, no doubt, but scarcely relevant to anyone's faith today. The buffoonery, the devils, a literal hell, even Mary as the Queen of Heaven, are trappings of medieval mystery plays which have no part in Oberammergau today. The single major non-biblical episode left in the play by Alois Daisenberger – that of Veronica wiping the face of Jesus on the way to Golgotha – disappeared in 1900.

The cluttered backstage area, which houses costumes and props and the actors' dressing-rooms, contrasts with the massive auditorium

Even so, some critics have cast doubts on the durability of the play in the final quarter of the twentieth century. *The Times*, again, cogently expressed this feeling during the season of 1980, when the newspaper's religious correspondent asked whether Oberammergau had reached 'the end of the line for biblical literalism'. He suggested that the Passion Play was now threatened because twentieth-century men and women could no longer accept what he called its 'naive view of the Gospels'. He admitted that the drama could still move some to tears. But, he argued, 'Modern biblical scholarship, entirely acceptable to the Roman Catholic authorities, has been ignored; the presentation is fundamentalist, and the Gospels taken at face value as accurate journalism.'

If this were true, then indeed the Oberammergau play might be threatened by what in the past many have regarded as its chief strength: its fidelity to Holy Scripture.

But the truth is that the Passion Play at Oberammergau by no means treats the Scriptures as journalism. No villager ever thought of them in such a way. Those who made their vow in 1633, those who have fulfilled it ever since – Ferdinand Rosner, Othmar Weiss, Alois Daisenberger and the countless others who have contributed to the play – regarded the Gospels as the supreme revelation of God.

Almost uncannily they saw their way to the heart of the Gospels in a manner remarkably confirmed by modern biblical scholars. The essence of the Gospels they perceived to be the passion story, that is, the narrative of how Jesus came to suffer (the Latin *passio* means 'suffering') and die.

Today scholars have come to see that the very earliest believers perceived this too. The earlier parts of the four Gospels differ in the way they treat the events in the life of Jesus, where they locate them in the narrative and how they interpret them. But when they come to the passion story, suddenly (as the German scholar Joachim Jeremias put it) the four Gospels present us with 'a close-packed, purposeful and coherent narrative'. This is what we see at Oberammergau.

The story of the passion, scholars now believe, was recited and remembered by the earliest Christians long before they put in order or wrote down any episodes from the rest of Jesus's life on earth. As another German scholar (Martin Kähler) put the matter 'somewhat provocatively', one could call the Gospels 'passion narratives with extended introductions'.

All this is not to pretend that the Oberammergauers were or are in some miraculous way scholars or university theologians. It is simply to assert that they instinctively perceived what was the heart of the Christian Gospel. Modern scholarship has confirmed what they saw, not demolished it.

Modern scholars, too, recognize what the play constantly proclaims: that there is a unity between the Old and the New Testaments. Those who wrote our Gospels needed to prove that what had happened to Jesus was all part of God's will. Since they believed God's will was revealed in the Old Testament, they never ceased to look there for parallels to what Jesus underwent in the last week of his life on earth. The older versions of the Passion Play used to do the same thing, with delightful literalness. Today a 'living tableau' of Joseph being sold by his brothers shows the Old Testament parallel to the betrayal of Jesus by Judas. But in the version of the play used until 1740, the enemies of Jesus actually say to Judas: 'We have at our disposal thirty pfennigs, old ones of good silver, for we have saved them for a long time. They are the coins for which Joseph was sold.'

Nowadays the Prologue simply sings, 'As Jacob's sons conspired against Joseph, soon you will hear these people rail wildly at the Saviour to demand his blood and death.'

The Passion Play is in such ways faithful to the Bible, but this is far from saying that it displays a naive literalness. Rather it mirrors the subtleties of Holy Scripture that are only now being rediscovered by modern scholars. And it does so in a way immediately accessible to thousands and thousands of visitors.

At the same time it presents, starkly and uncluttered by any medieval allegories or theatrical frills, the uniqueness of Jesus's death on the cross. The Romans crucified countless Jews in their brief period of military and civil occupation of the Holy Land. None had the effect on the world of the crucifixion of Jesus of Nazareth. The play finds parallels in the Old Testament for Jesus's agony in the garden of Gethsemane. 'As Adam toils, pressured by life's hardships, his forces spent, sweat on his brow, to atone his own sin,' the Prologue sings, 'thus the sins of others press on our Saviour.' And the 'living tableau' of Moses raising the serpent in the wilderness is seen to prefigure the crucifixion. Before that episode the

Jesus, played by Anton Preisinger, appears in the 1950 production

Old Testament parallels suddenly disappear from the Oberammergau stage. As Hermine Diemer put it, 'There is no allegorical picture to precede this presentation. What we are about to witness is so terrible that no symbol of the Old Testament would be grand and weighty enough to put before the expiation of the Son of God.'

The distinguished historian Algernon Cecil, after visiting Oberammergau, wrote: 'It seems to be a postulate of any credible narrative of the life of Christ that this should be the work of simple people.' He misunderstood both the evangelists from whom we have our Gospels and the Oberammergauers whose Passion Play he was responding to.

The evangelists were not twentieth-century men, but they were no less intelligent than ourselves and they were inspired as few have been before or since. The people of Oberammergau who created the Passion Play knew nothing of twentieth-century civilization, but this did not make them simple rustics. Hermine Diemer, who knew them better than Algernon Cecil, noted with some acerbity that even people who should know better 'often make the mistake of taking the Oberammergauers for primitive rustic characters, ascribing the certain refinements they come across in dealing with them to influences from without'.

It is a small step from this judgement to the equally erroneous assumption that the Passion Play created by these 'primitive rustic characters' is fit only for unsophisticated peasants, and not for cultivated twentieth-century men and women. Montrose J. Moses came close to such a judgement in 1910. 'Because of the very fact that the people of Oberammergau are aloof, simple, childlike in belief and imbued with an inherited mission,' he wrote, 'because they have elected to do one thing and to subserve all else to that one thing, the spirit in which they preserve their institution is what makes the Passion Play a living force – to them.'

Since he wrote those words, the Passion Play has remained a living force for millions of others. Not all of them have been 'believers' in the usual way believers are defined. Algernon Cecil very neatly described the diverse characters that crowd into Oberammergau during the play seasons. He saw 'Dives, who has made his pile and is trying to enjoy it; Herod, who is curious to inspect every fresh manifestation of the supernatural; Gallio, who ... cared for none of these things'. He saw the professor 'who has disproved the very existence of what he has come to see – and Uncertainty, writ large upon the vast crowd of human creatures who are neither for God nor against Him'.

The point, as Eduard Devrient put it, is 'to come, to see, to learn'. After quoting those words, Hans Andersen told of the effect made by the Oberammergau Passion Play on him. As a Danish Protestant he had come with some doubts. Afterwards he confessed, 'Never shall I forget the Passion Play at Oberammergau, so completely did it surpass all my expectation. I could not think of it beforehand without being scandalized at the idea of seeing Jesus acted on the stage; but as it here took place, in religious faith, full of fervour, all offence was taken away.' He added: 'The whole religious play has a majesty, a simplicity, something so strangely absorbing that even the most irreligious must needs be dumb.'

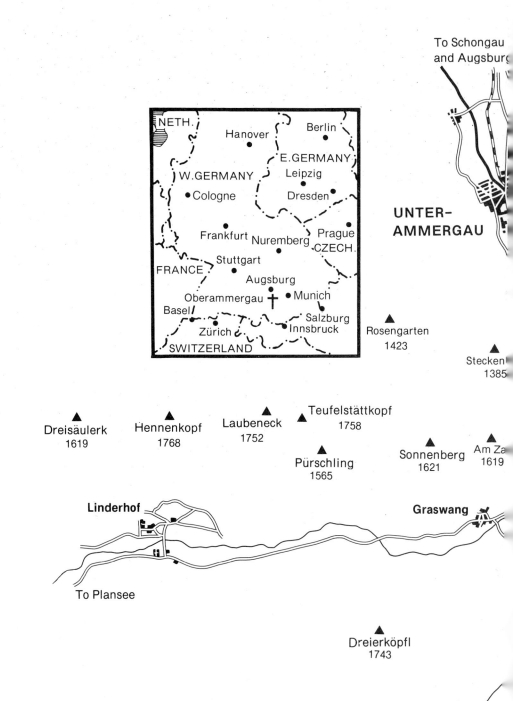

NETH.

Hanover

Berlin

E.GERMANY

W.GERMANY

Leipzig

Cologne

Dresden

Frankfurt

Nuremberg

Prague

CZECH.

Stuttgart

FRANCE

Augsburg

Oberammergau

Munich

Basel

Salzburg

Zürich

Innsbruck

SWITZERLAND

To Schongau
and Augsburg

UNTER-
AMMERGAU

▲ Rosengarten
1423

▲ Stecken
1385

▲ Dreisäulerk
1619

▲ Hennenkopf
1768

▲ Laubeneck
1752

▲ Teufelstättkopf
1758

▲ Pürschling
1565

▲ Sonnenberg
1621

▲ Am Za
1619

Linderhof

Graswang

To Plansee

▲ Dreierköpfl
1743

▲ Kuchelberg Spitz
2022

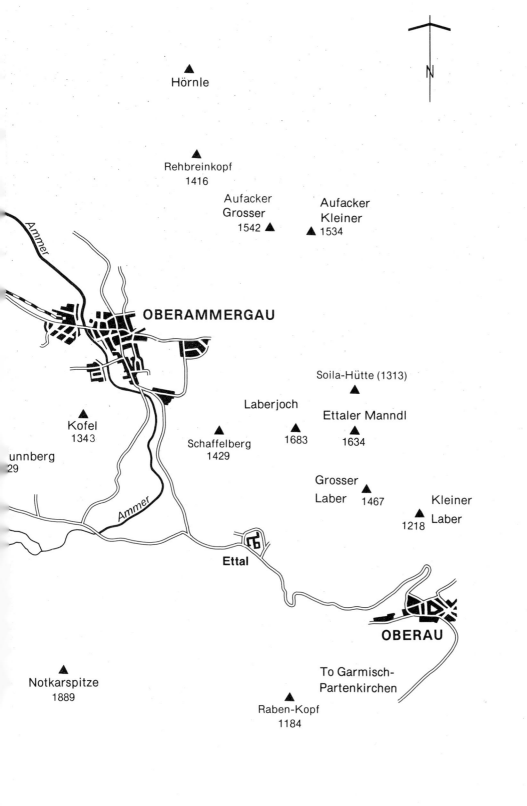

Hörnle

N

Rehbreinkopf
1416

Aufacker
Grosser
1542 ▲   Aufacker
             Kleiner
         ▲ 1534

Ammer

OBERAMMERGAU

Soila-Hütte (1313)
▲

Laberjoch

Ettaler Manndl

Kofel
1343   Schaffelberg   ▲   ▲
            1429   1683   1634

unnberg
29

                    Grosser   ▲
                    Laber   1467   Kleiner
Ammer   ▲ Laber
                                    1218

Ettal

OBERAU

Notkarspitze
1889   To Garmisch-
                    Partenkirchen
            Raben-Kopf
            1184

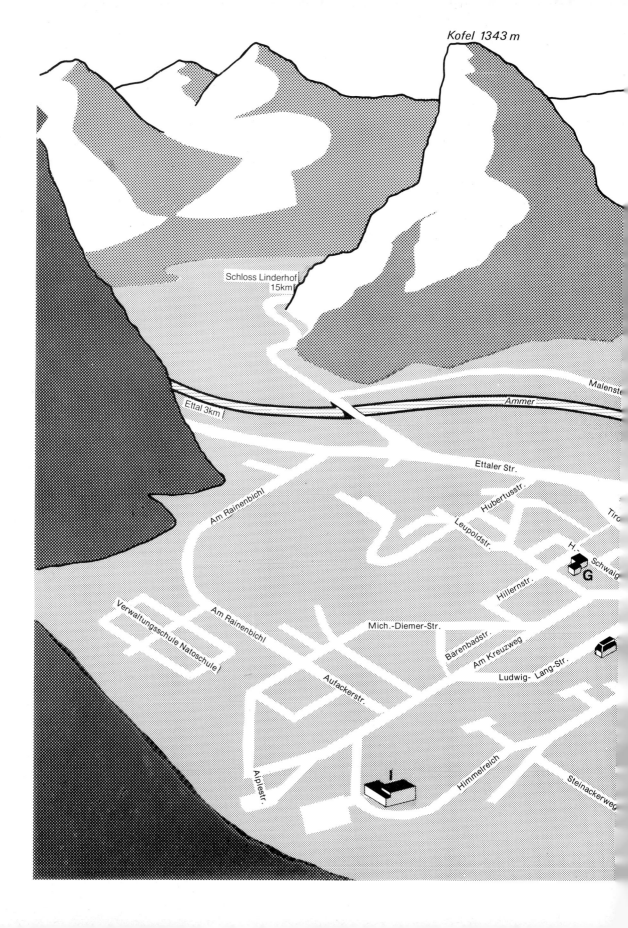

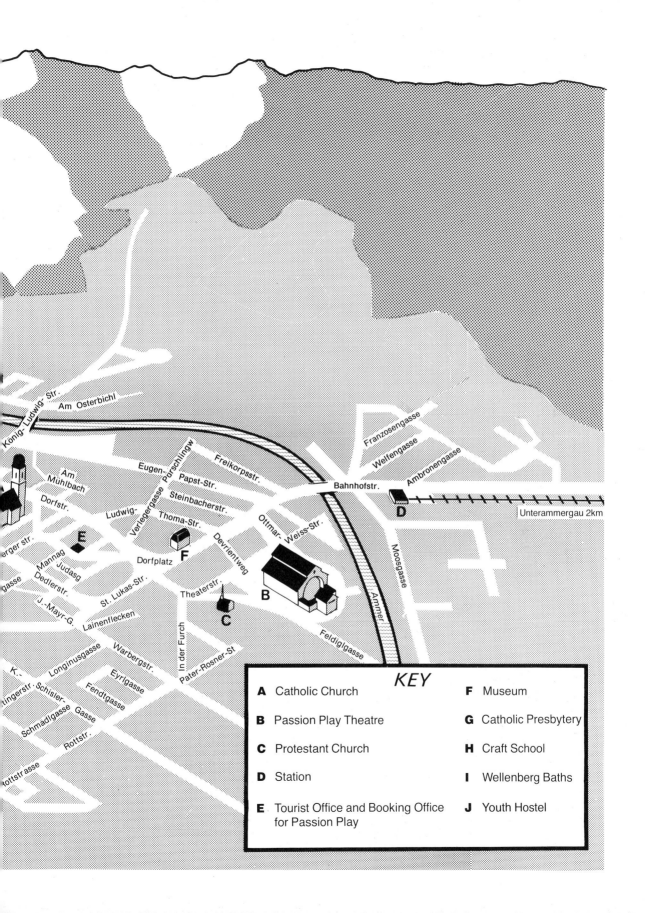

König-Ludwig-Str.

Am Osterbichl

Eugen-Papst-Str.

Porschingw.

Freikorpsstr.

Franzosengasse

Welfengasse

Ambronengasse

Bahnhofstr.

Am Mühlbach

Dorfstr.

Ludwig-

Vertegergasse

Steinbacherstr.

Thoma-Str.

D

Unterammergau 2km

E

Mannag

Judasg.

Dedlerstr.

Dorfplatz

F

Devrientweg

Ottmar-Weiss-Str.

Moosgasse

J.-Mayr-G.

St. Lukas-Str.

Theaterstr.

C

B

Ammer

Lainenflecken

In der Furch

Longinusgasse

Warbergstr.

Pater-Rosner-St

Feldiglgasse

Eyrlgasse

Fendlgasse

Schisler-Gasse

Schmadlgasse

Rottstr.

Rottstrasse

KEY

A Catholic Church

B Passion Play Theatre

C Protestant Church

D Station

E Tourist Office and Booking Office
for Passion Play

F Museum

G Catholic Presbytery

H Craft School

I Wellenberg Baths

J Youth Hostel

Further Reading

To research and write this book gave me a great deal of pleasure, and some readers, too, might enjoy pursuing certain themes.

First published in 1891 and still in print is Jerome K. Jerome's *Diary of a Pilgrimage*, a hilarious yet reverent account of his journey with a stockbroker friend to Oberammergau for the passion play of 1890. The description of the same production by the crusading journalist W. T. Stead was published in 1891 as *The Story that Transformed the World*. F. W. Farrar, Dean of Canterbury, novelist and popular theologian, was also inspired by that year's production to write *The Passion Play at Oberammergau*. And by now the play was so widely acclaimed inside and outside Germany as to warrant a full edition of Pastor Alois Daisenberger's *Text des Oberammergauer Passionsspieles*, published in Munich in 1890 by H. Korff.

The impact of the passion play on mid-nineteenth-century Germany is best illustrated by Eduard Devrient's *Das Passion Schauspiel im Dorfe Oberammergau in Oberbauern* (J. J. Weber, Leipzig, 1851). You can read Hans Christian Andersen's charming response to the 1860 season in his *Pictures of Travel* (Hurd & Houghton, New York, 1871). In 1870 Canon Malcolm MacColl's *The Ammergau Passion Play* popularized the play for British readers and gave prospective visitors hints on getting there. Ten years later Mary Frances Drew provided a competent translation, entitled *The Passion Play at Oberammergau: the Great Atonement at Golgotha*.

Musicians will relish F. Schoeberl's *The Passion Play of Oberammergau, with Special Reference to its Musical Beauties*, published in 1874, and Robert Muenster's 1970 study, *Rochus Dedler, 1779-1822*. Those who would like to trace the development of today's play from its earliest origins should consult the edition of the 1662 text in Guido Lang, *Der älteste Text des Oberammergauer Passionsspieles* (G. Lang, Oberammergau, 1910), and Stephen Schaller's edition of Ferdinand Rosner's eighteenth-century version, *Passio nova: das Oberammergauer Passionsspiel von 1750* (Geistliche Texte des 17. und 18. Jahrhunderts, Band I, Bern, 1974).

Interesting accounts of twentieth-century Oberammergau seasons include Montrose J. Moses' *The Passion Play of Oberammergau* (Duffield & Co., New York, 1910), Ernest Hermitage Day's *Ober-Ammergau and its Passion Play* (1910), which has some fascinating information about tourism, Algernon Cecil's account of the 1922 season (published in *A Dreamer in Christendom*, 1925), and Hermine Diemer's *Oberammergau and its Passion Play* (4th edition, Carl Schnell & Söhne, Munich, 1930), which is filled with delightful descriptions of local Oberammergau customs.

The Jubilee Text of the 1934 season is available in English (J. C. Huber, Diessen vor München, 1934). Elisabethe Corathiel's account of Anton Lang's sufferings under the Hitler regime, and of the difficulties faced by Oberammergau after the Second World War, are found in her *Oberammergau and its Passion Play* (1950).

Finally, Wilfrid Blunt's *The Dream King* (Penguin, 1973) is a lavishly illustrated account of the tragic life and fabulous castles of King Ludwig II, and *Baroque and Rococo*, edited by A. Blunt (1978), contains fine photographs of some of the splendid churches around Oberammergau.

Index